CONFLICTED

ALICE LA ROUX & M.S.L.R

Copyright © 2017 Alice La Roux & M.S.L.R

Cover Design: Emma Louise
Editing: A. T. Sullivan
Formatting: JC Clarke
All Rights Reserved.

No part of this book may be reproduced in any form or by any electronic or mechanical means without written permission from the author.

This is a work of fiction. The names, places, characters are all a work of fiction. Any resemblance to persons, living or dead, events or businesses are entirely coincidental.

Please be aware that this book was co-authored by a British and an America writer.

There may be some discrepancies or variations in spelling although we have tried to limit this.

The use of 'mum' instead of 'mom' in places is intentional.

PLAYLIST

Wet – Don't Wanna Be Your Girl
Leona Lewis – Bleeding Love
Usher – Burn
Fallulah – Give Us A Little Love
Adele – Set Fire To The Rain
Chicane feat. Tom Jones – Stoned In Love
Ellie Goulding – Love Me Like You Do
Katy Perry – The One That Got Away
Nick Jonas feat. Tove Lo – Close
Ed Sheeran – Shape Of You
Lorde – Green Light
Gotye – Hearts A Mess
Alex Clare – Too Close

KALEB

Prologue

It wasn't what I wanted, but I had to go. I had to leave this life, I *needed* to leave her— it was the only way.

When she walked into the room, my eyes met hers. I'd always thought that Serena Davies was gorgeous, with her long dark hair streaked through with blue, purple, and red. She had these honey colored eyes that saw right through me. Serena was a wild beauty, which was unsurprising given her Welsh heritage. Together we made a striking pair, with my short dark hair and blue eyes. I was tanned, but only because I grew up in Los Angeles, California. Surfing used to be my way of life— plus my tattoos looked better that way. "You're here." It wasn't a question, but I nodded anyway.

It was late, almost midnight. We'd both left work in our own separate cars, nobody ever suspected a thing. We both knew it was wrong, but we couldn't help it. I sat on the bed in our room at the Holiday Inn. We had promised to stay away from each. At work we avoided one another, not that anyone would really notice since we didn't actually work together all that much.

She placed her purse down slowly before walking towards me, but didn't get too close.

"I know we promised, but after earlier..." she didn't have to say it. We both knew that it would be hard.

We both happened to answer a call at work, a customer wanted to know if we had a certain brand of coffee maker in stock. I hadn't realized that Serena had answered the call before I did, the customer hadn't mentioned it. So when I couldn't find the coffee maker on the floor I had to look in the stock room and that's where I found Serena already searching for it.

She hadn't seen me at first. She was bent over looking underneath a shelf but there weren't any there. We were sold out.

"Are you looking for the coffee maker too?" I startled her.

She almost bumped her head as she stood up. "God, don't do that." she almost smiled, but cleared her throat instead. "Yeah, um...we're out. I think."

I came closer and glanced quickly underneath the shelf, but I already knew there weren't any.

"I guess we are." we stood awkwardly for a moment.

"Maybe I—" I started.

"So ho—" we spoke at the same time.

We both laughed.

It had been at least two weeks since the last time we had seen each other. We had ended things then but I still wanted her.

"So how's Jen?" She asked. Jen was my girlfriend, we had been dating for over two years now but then I met Serena, and everything changed. It was like my world had shifted. Being with Serena had made me realize that Jen and I had never had that spark.

"Fine, and Sean?" I asked in return. Sean was her boyfriend and they had been together far longer than Jen and I had, about six years. He wanted to marry her, and that made my chest ache whenever I thought about it.

"Good." she looked away. "I think I should go and tell the customer we're out."

Without thinking I grabbed hold of her arm as she started to walk past me. "I miss you." I said as I pulled her into me, she didn't push me away. Our bodies were meant for each other, hers fit perfectly against mine.

"Kaleb," she whispered. "We promised we wouldn't do this again."

But what would you do if you knew you weren't with the love of your life? What if there wasn't much you could do about it, because you were in a committed relationship for years now and still cared for that person? What could you do then?

We were both in that situation; Serena was in an even harder place. She was practically engaged, but she wasn't really in love with him, although she would never admit it. They had been together for so long, they were used to each other. That was one of the reasons why I had to go.

There was no kissing, we just held each other. I had my arms around her and she had hers around me; we were like a Celtic knot, unsure of where one began and the other ended. We stayed like that for a moment or two. Until we were interrupted.

"Kaleb call 101, Kaleb call 101." came the voice over the intercom.

I sighed. That was our cue to go.

Slowly we disentangled from one another. "The

usual?" she asked as she turned to leave. I knew what that meant, she didn't have to explain.

For a moment I hesitated, but then nodded.

And that was how we ended up back at the hotel, meeting in secrecy again. Jen and Sean didn't deserve this, another reason why I *had* to leave. *For good.*

About a month ago I was offered a higher position back in Los Angeles but I had declined it. A few days ago I got a call from the same store but this time I'd told them I would think about it. Maybe putting some distance between us would make things easier, I hadn't accepted the offer, but I was going to.

I stood up. "Serena, about the job offer I got before— remember I told you about it?"

She nodded. "Yeah, what about it?" her face told me she knew where I was going with this, but I said it anyway.

"I'm going to accept it. I'm leaving San Francisco." To myself I sounded firm and strong about the decision I had made, but that wasn't how I really felt about it. It just had to happen.

I wasn't sure what kind of reaction I had expected from her. She just stared at me.

"Are you okay?" I came closer.

She looked away, a tear ran down her face, and then more came. But she didn't wipe them away.

"I knew one of us was going to have to do something drastic. I'm just not strong enough to…end it, to leave you."

I couldn't help it, and hugged her. "I'm sorry." I said, "I wish it was easier. But if I stay, I'm not going to be able to stay away from you. Do you understand that?" It was the truth. "If I stayed I would ruin both of our relationships and you would resent me forever. I'm not going to risk that."

We had never discussed how we felt about each other. When all of this had started it had just been about sex. There was an intense attraction we had towards each other from the very beginning. I could see now that we were each other's better half and if it had been a different time, we would probably be happy together. Unfortunately that wasn't the case.

But it couldn't last forever. Reality happened. Sean had begun to get suspicious so we stopped meeting. Seeing her today though, there were no words to describe how I felt.

"Kaleb, I want you to know that I—" she began but I couldn't let her finish. So my mouth met hers and it was a gentle kiss, I poured all the love I felt into it.

I knew what she was going to say but I couldn't hear it, I couldn't let her say it now. "Shh, don't" I whispered. "If you say it, I won't be able to leave." At the same time, I wished she had said it. That would break that invisible barrier that was standing between us. That would have made this real. That would have brought us together once and for all.

But she hadn't said it.

Just like I had to leave, she couldn't say it.

We kissed one last time before I grabbed my coat.

"Will I see you again?" she said, hugging herself. Even with her smeared makeup, she was still beautiful.

My eyes were teary, I knew and didn't care. "I don't know." I said honestly. "Good bye Serena." She hugged me one last time.

I gave her a kiss on the forehead and then walked out of the hotel room.

One Year Later

I look at the flashy diamond on my left hand, cringing every time it catches the light and glistens. I said yes. Why did I say yes? I look over at Sean, laughing with his father before pulling my mother into a hug. Happiness radiates from his face, but all I feel is this deep sense of guilt gnawing away at me. It had been the right decision, the next step, as everyone kept saying— only logical. Then why did I feel like I'd swallowed a golf ball, or like there was a collar clasped around my neck? I feel like there is something trying to cut off my voice so that when I whispered 'yes' it hadn't even felt real.

The guilt keeps eating at me and finally I excuse myself from the restaurant and both our families to go to the bathroom. He'd planned all of this very carefully, inviting both sets of parents out for dinner so they could witness as he asked me to be his forever.

Looking at myself in the mirror I could see the old me, the me before Kaleb. I looked the same but I didn't feel the same. This wasn't me, not anymore. I splash a little cold water on my face, telling myself that I have to get a grip. My life was good, I'd been made a Team Leader at work, we'd just put an offer in on a house and I was newly engaged. I didn't have time to think about Kaleb, or wonder how he was.

When he'd left, when he called it quits between us, I'd been on the verge of telling him that I loved him. The words were there, about to tumble from my lips and change my life, but he'd stopped me. He didn't want my love and in the same breath he told me he was leaving. To say I was crushed was an understatement. I'd been so broken hearted it had been impossible to hide and Sean became worried about me. It had taken me months to get myself back together, collecting all the little broken pieces and trying to be the same old me. I'd made a great friend named Laura in my yoga class. I was getting my life on track and everything was as it should be, but for some reason this engagement had floored me. It had made me stop and really think. I could feel the sadness seeping from the cracks of the life I was struggling to hold together. I hold my hands up to my mouth to stop the sob I can feel rising in my chest, the diamond from my ring cutting into my other palm. I'd almost forgotten about the ring.

Slowly my hands fall down by my sides. This isn't a bad thing. I loved Sean. He had always been there for me, supported me, loved me unconditionally. He was safe. I would never have to worry about him hurting me or leaving me. He was comfortable and I knew realistically I'd be happy with him, in our perfect house with our perfect children. Taking a deep breath I swallow the sob, straighten my shoulders and smooth down my dress. I would make this work—Sean deserved his happily ever after. This would work.

KALEB

It had been exactly a year.

A year in which I had to keep myself so busy working hard just so I wouldn't think about her. But now— it was quiet and I hated down times like this. I was at home, alone. Jen was still at work and would be until late. We hardly ever saw each other but that didn't bother me at all. Although I didn't like the alone time, I probably disliked spending time with her more.

I knew that wasn't a good sign.

In fact, I had a feeling she was cheating on me but even that didn't bother me so much. Ever since I suspected it, I stopped sleeping with her. It'd been a couple of months now. Even though there were moments of loneliness for me, I couldn't do it. I couldn't make myself love her, no matter how hard we both tried.

I knew she wasn't happy with me and so whoever she was seeing now would probably treat her better.

No – they would *definitely* treat her better. I was just waiting for her to make that decision and leave. She'd relocated for me, given up her job for me and I couldn't be the one to end things. She deserved a shot at happiness and when she realized that, I'd let her go without a fight. Not that I condone cheating but who were we kidding? I'd done it before and still would be if we hadn't moved.

See? There I went again thinking about her.

Serena.

I pulled out my laptop and searched for her on Facebook. It may have seemed creepy and felt a little like I was stalking her, but I just wanted to know how she was doing. Her profile came up and I stared at her picture. She was so gorgeous, even more than I had remembered. Her smile gives me a twinge of sadness because I wasn't the one behind the camera making her laugh.

Slowly I scrolled down her page and saw from her last post that had a check in at some spa. Good, Serena always worked too hard, trying to climb her way to a promotion. She needed the time to pamper herself.

How did I know that?

I'd been keeping tabs on her. Not because I was obsessed, I mean you could say in a way I was, but she was *The One*. I wanted her and now I knew it would always be her. If it hadn't been for certain people, I wouldn't have walked away. But that didn't stop me from doubting the decision I'd made a year ago. I wish I'd been stronger, more selfish. I wish that things had been different.

Several times I thought about calling her or even just writing her a simple letter to explain things, and let her know I was thinking about her. But I never went through with it. For one, she seemed happy. Two, she was still with Sean which meant that my decision to leave was the right move. She was happy with him before me, she could be happy again if I gave her time.

But somehow I hoped that she felt the same way and still thought about me too.

Serena

THREE YEARS LATER

I jitter my legs nervously again— I can't seem to keep still, every cell in my body is trembling. I bite my nails, a disgusting habit that only emerges when I get stressed. I check my watch and groan softly when I realize it's only ten past eleven and my interview is at twenty past. That's ten more minutes of jitteriness and fidgeting. Today I'm a bag of nerves and I can't help it. Deciding to kill some time by reapplying my makeup, I head to the bathroom.

I have to make a good impression, I need this job. Things have been tight money wise, what with the new house and Sean hinting again that he'd like to start a family. Babies cost money, at least that's the reason I give him for putting it off. That and the fact that we still aren't married yet, another topic I've been avoiding. I just can't bring myself to plan anything, to commit to a date, a color scheme or venue. I don't care about roses, daisies or peonies. I'm indifferent to it all; the excitement that other brides seem to have just doesn't affect me. Does that mean there's something wrong with me? I shake away the thought and focus.

I look in the mirror, my long dark hair flows down past my shoulders, hints of red catching in the light. I look tired, but nothing a bit of concealer won't fix. I pull a dark red lipstick out from my purse. I want to look professional but I also want to wow them, I think as I smear it across my full, plump lips. I'd always felt self-conscious about them because I always look like I'm pouting, but Sean said it was one of my best features. Pushing all thoughts of him away I smile sweetly at my reflection.

This interview is important and I know I shouldn't be so worried because I'm an internal candidate— but I am. It would mean moving to a brand new store and starting from scratch, but as a trainee manager rather than a team leader or a sales assistant. I'd been trying to move up and finally I had a shot— I wasn't going to waste it. It had taken me hours of agonizing over what to wear and I'd finally gone with a fitted white blouse that's nipped in at the waist, with a knee length pencil skirt and a pair of smart black heels. I look both sexy and refined, how could they possibly say no? Exhaling the breath I didn't realize I'd been holding in slowly, I go back to the waiting area to be called, there are only two minutes left now. I'm being interviewed by a panel of three senior managers, one of whom I'll be working with closely if I get the job. I take another deep breath as my name is called and head into the conference room. I can do this I tell myself as I smile and look up to shake hands with my interviewers.

It's him. I falter, my heart hammering in my chest. It's him. He's back. Standing before me in a crisp navy suit, his blue eyes look me up and down, pausing briefly on my legs. He always did love my legs, especially when they were wrapped around his waist. Images of the two us entwined flood my mind and I can't breathe. His olive skin is darker; he's been somewhere sunny recently and I feel a pang of jealousy that I wasn't there with him. My eyes trail over the new tattoos creeping out from under the collar of his white shirt up the side of his neck. My fingers itch to reach out and touch them, to feel the warmth of his body beneath mine. Kaleb Collins hasn't changed and for some reason that makes me angry. Maybe it's because it was so easy for him to leave me three years ago. Or maybe it's because I'm still attracted to him. He holds out his hand, flashing me that sinful grin of his and I can feel my face beginning to burn. I slip my hand into his and shake it. The electricity that passes between us as we touch is palpable.

I loved Sean. I did. What we had was good and stable. It was the kind of relationship that you settle down and eventually raise a family in. Sean was white picket fences, rockers on the porch and that feeling of being safe when you crawled into bed after a long day. But Kaleb set my soul on fire. He made my heart beat race with every touch, every glance, and every kiss. Seeing him now I know that nothing has changed, he still makes my knees go weak and my skin tingle.

I lick my lips, my mouth suddenly dry and it's like I've forgotten how to speak. I nod and smile at the other interviewers, one of which is an older woman with blonde hair and a stern face. The other is a gentleman in his fifties with greying hair, kind eyes and a round belly. I sit crossing my legs carefully.

Kaleb's eyes never leave mine and it's like we're the only two in the room.

I can't believe he is one of the panelists— fate really has it out for me by putting him in my path once again. Especially when I've spent the last couple of years trying to get over him. I try so hard to resist him but I can never stay away. Kaleb was a force to be reckoned with, an uncontrollable storm and I am lost to him already.

KALEB

I know who's going to walk through my office door before the interview is even confirmed. *Serena is going to work for me.* It's something that I've already decided but we still have to go through the hiring process.

She has to do the interview because that's company policy, but I'd hire her on the spot if it didn't make me look so desperate. So I have to pretend to be surprised when I see her, our eyes locking into place as soon as she looks up. It is the moment of truth, and I can feel my heart hammering so loudly it's like she's walking to its beat as she enters the room.

I take her hand briefly and then step away. I can tell I've shaken her as it takes her a moment or two to notice the other people in the room. The other interviewers, Carys and Marshall, are leaving and I can feel myself growing impatient as they introduce themselves to her before they go. We all agreed to take turns interviewing candidates and this time it was mine. Of course I'd planned all of this ahead of time, I wasn't about to let her go a second time. My eyes never leave her as she makes her way back to me.

"Serena." I say coolly.

She smiles and nods but doesn't say anything back. I can tell she is nervous and seeing me again, here of all places, she's desperately trying to process the situation. The way her face furrows, those cute little lines between her brows, confirms this. I know I just have to give her a minute but then we'd talk.

With that outfit she's wearing it's not all I really have in mind though. She may have changed her wardrobe and even her hair but then honestly, so had I, and I couldn't wait to show off the more serious, polished Kaleb that I'd been working on during our time apart. We weren't the same people but there's still this connection— an undeniable spark. I could feel it, and something told me she could too. The thought made me smile.

"Take a seat" I say as I motion to a chair.

She walks in front of me swaying her hips from side to side and holy fuck, that pencil skirt hugs her lower body in all the right places. As I take my own seat opposite her I look away trying to clear my mind of dirty thoughts.

"It's been a long time," She says, her voice, sweet and calm as if I hadn't shocked her into silence just a moment ago.

I nod.

"It has," but it really hasn't since I've been keeping tabs on her because I missed her in more ways than one, but I keep that to myself, "As you can see we're looking for someone to join the team. We're growing and moving fast, so with that comes new hires. My team has selected a few candidates to interview for this position you're interested in. You would be working directly for me and with me. I don't want to hear why you think you're good for this role but rather I want to know what you can bring to the table."

It was plain and simple really. Even if the others had to interview Serena, I knew she would nail it because of her personality and her experience. Looking at the other resumes, I knew they would be good options as well but I didn't know them like I knew her, and she is a hard working woman, someone I know I could trust.

Serena didn't quite smile but gave me a firm nod before she spoke, "Besides experience, I can bring creativity and new ideas to help with the growth of this business. Since I'm looking for a role where I can move up, this is ideal for me and it's why I'm here."

"Good, I'm sure you'd be an asset to the team." I say confidently but in my mind her beauty is distracting me and I'm struggling to keep everything professional.

It wasn't just the physical attraction but something more, there's always been more with Serena. She meant more to me than anyone ever had, I never forgot that and she didn't know...

As we talk, I picture her on top of my desk, down to her panties and that white dress shirt unbuttoned, her legs spread apart in front me, saying my name over and over again. I know it's only a fantasy but I was determined to make it happen. *Soon.*

"Why are you back?" The way she says that quickly shatters my filthy thoughts and brings me back to reality. I haven't asked anything since her reply to my question and now we're off track.

Serena is unlike any other women I've been with, Jen included. It would've been foolish of me to think she wouldn't want to know why I was back in town after I had promised I'd stay away. So of course, it would come up sooner or later.

I move her resume into a folder and set it aside as I face her questioning eyes. There is no point in continuing to ask her these stupid questions when I knew everything about her.

"Why do you think?" My bluntness makes her look away, "I'm where I want to be in my career and it's brought me back here, which is a plus in my book."

She glances back at me and then away again, keeping her eyes trained on something else.

"Do you think you can do it?" I ask because I want to know that she's going to take the job, she has to. "Do you think you can work here, so close to me again?" There's no point in sugar coating it, either she would or wouldn't.

"Yes. I can. It would be my job and I'm a professional at all times." She moves a strand of hair behind her ear but tries to keep an icy look on her face. She's trying to act like I wasn't affecting her at all.

We'd see about that.

"Hmm, I don't know that you will be able to stay professional Serena. Maybe that's what you want to think." I grin, "You may not have what it takes to—"

Serena stands up, "Stop Kaleb. We're not those people anymore. I don't know if you're teasing me but this isn't a joke. *This* is my life." She leans over my desk with her hands on either side, her face serious and this time I wasn't sure whether the iciness in her eyes was a bluff.

I have pushed her enough, "It's *both* our lives and you would fit in, here with us," It's the honest truth, "But I won't stop Serena because we have unfinished business here, you feel something. Something you've never let go of and neither have I. The question is can you handle that?"

Serena has stepped away as I stand up and tower over her, she's overwhelmed and that's the point. I want to invade her space, her mind, her body and eventually I'll have her heart.

Surprising me, she grabs her purse and walks towards the door.

"Do you feel anything for me?" My voice is loud enough for her to hear even though she's already across the room, but I can't hold myself back now. I'm an alpha male no doubt, but if there were ever a woman that could hold my heart in her hand, it'd be her. The words were out of my mouth before I could think about it.

She turns with a sad look on her face that I wish I could permanently erase.

"What do you want me to say? It's been three years Kaleb. It's not fair for you to come back and open old wounds up again." She looks away.

I knew it. Although she's right and I want to change our situation so we could have a chance at a future together, I knew I hurt her when I left but I could also see there was hope. She wouldn't be so upset if she didn't care.

A few moments of silence passed between us before she turns around and starts to open the door.

"We'll be making a decision soon. It was lovely seeing you again Serena." I'm back to my serious self and I really can't wait for her to so start working with me.

She nods, and leaves without looking back.

Serena

So I got the job. The phone call came a few hours after I left the interview and instead of feeling excited, I felt nervous. Could I work with Kaleb? I fired off a quick text to Sean, we were having dinner at his mother's tonight and I just needed some space to think. I got off the bus at a park near our house and sat on the bench by myself. I felt like I was bursting at the seams with emotion, nothing felt comfortable or safe, instead I felt like crawling out of my skin. When the light started to fade and I'd decided that I was going to make this new job work— no matter what Kaleb tried to throw at me, I walked home. Sean had already gone to his mother's, leaving a note to say he'd be waiting for me there. I took a deep breath and changed into a royal blue bodycon dress that I loved. I needed to feel confident and clothes were my armor.

Sean's mother, Shelby, called out at me to 'Come in' when I'd knocked on the door. I walked through into the house and realized that she must have guests as there were several coats hung up by the door. I follow the sound of laughter into the dining room where Sean, his parents, my parents, my best friend Laura, and Sean's brother were all seated around the table, pouring wine and chatting. I cringed when I saw a cake, emblazoned with 'Congrats!' in bright pink icing sat off to the side. He had thrown me a dinner party for getting the job, a job working for the man I'd had an affair with. They all turned to face me, offering their own congratulatory messages and my parents stood to hug me.

"You're a bit overdressed aren't you?" Sean whispered in my ear as he wrapped an arm around my waist and kissed my cheek.

"I like this dress." I said calmly.

He shrugged and any confidence I had drained out of me, leaving me feel deflated and flat. "It's a little revealing don't you think?" He says finally before going to pour himself another glass of wine.

Laura came up to me next and pulled me into a tight squish. "What did dickwad say to you?"

"He doesn't like my dress. He thinks it's a bit much."

She pulls away and rubs my arm, giving me that pitying look she does sometimes. She hated Sean and nothing I said would ever change that. "You know that he puts you down on purpose, don't you?"

"No— he's not like that Lau. He's right. It's just dinner."

"It's a celebratory dinner Serena. We are here to celebrate you— that means you can wear whatever the fuck you like." She frowns, she's never gotten along with Sean but she doesn't see him the way I do. She doesn't know the real him and I can't hold that against her.

"Besides, look at his mother. If that isn't mutton dressed as lamb I don't know what is."

We both turn to look at Shelby, her blonde hair brushed to cover the bald spot that was still visible at the back of her head. As if she knew we were discussing her, she pulled out a small pocket mirror and reapplied the red lipstick that was several shades too bright for her pale skin. Putting the mirror away she smoothed down her yellow sundress, which was too short for a woman of her age. I always admired her dress sense thinking that she just wore what she wanted, but as I watched closely I saw Sean's father lean in, his hand on her waist mirroring what Sean had just done to me. Her face may not have dropped like mine, but her smile grew smaller and tighter like she was forcing it.

"When will you see it Rena?" Laura's sad eyes made me want to cry, but Sean was good to me. He'd always been there for me, taken care of me and he loved me. I needed him.

"So Serena sweetie, what's your new boss like?" my mother asked as we dished out dessert, the roast beef dinner that Shelby had spent all afternoon cooking had been demolished and now we'd moved onto the cake.

"You've met him mum, I used to work with him before."

Next to me Sean stilled in his seat, it was like he knew what I was going to say before I even said it. But he didn't know about our affair, did he?

"Kaleb— remember, he came to that staff barbeque a few years ago, and he was at the charity night you organized."

"Ahhh. Yes, Kaleb." She says and her tone is clipped. The atmosphere in the room becomes stifling as a silence settles over us.

KALEB

I have "friends" but we're not really close. Back when I was in school, I was a loner, instead preferring my own company but I quickly realized I had make some changes if I wanted be successful in my career. Networking became a must. Sure enough, it helped in the long run. Through college and when I left, I was well respected. Not to brag, but, I was the one everyone was jealous of for one reason or another and to be honest, that was fine with me. I didn't need anyone. You could call it arrogance but I say it was more a rebellious attitude than anything else.

It all started with my parents, they both came from Old Money. Achievements and recognition meant a lot to them, so they always encouraged my older brother and I. Don't think that means they didn't love us, they did, they just also believed in pushing us to be the best. My brother, Christian, is also good at everything he does. We're both competitive, it's just how we are, how we've always been. He's an architect and lives in New York with his pretty wife and small yappy dog. He's the big shot there. We're family but we can't be around each other for long, because we can't help but try and one up each other on everything.

Managing a store doesn't sound like I'm at the top of my game, and that's because it isn't. I decided after college to rebel and as a result I took a menial job in a store. I worked the stockroom to begin with, and then I found that I loved it. Working my way up made me feel like I'd accomplished something, and doing it without my parents name or money was a bonus. The shitty wage didn't even matter, it was like pocket change after the money I received when my grandfather died. The plan was to one day open my own place, using everything I'd learned here.

So for now I'm alone here in San Francisco, no Jen to act as my social networker but I do know a few people from when I lived here before. I have acquaintances, a lot of them in fact, and right now I'm surrounded as I take a shot of tequila because it's been a long fucking frustrating day.

Serena doesn't know what I had to go through to make sure she got the job. It's not because she's not good enough or because of her resume, truthfully it's because of me. I know Ceci, an ex-fling of mine, had something to do with HR questioning me like I was some kind of predator for wanting a beautiful woman working for me. That wasn't the case at all, I knew Serena personally, I trusted her – not that it was any of their business. Even though they had already told her that she got the job, they had "concerns" they wanted to address with me before she officially started. It was complete bullshit.

"You seem out of it man." One of the guys from work – Matt, I think his name is but I can't be sure – comments and gives me an odd look.

I shrug because this time I'm not there to play poker or have a conversation about sports or whatever, just need a drink or two to wash away the day and then I'll be on my way home.

"Rough day at work?" Says another, who I don't really know.

"Just had a lot to do today." It's the only answer I give but they seem satisfied enough and go back to their conversation. I try to do my best to join in on the banter and have some fun but there's just too much on my mind to have a good time. I can't be social and charming guy I usually am right now – it's all too much effort.

I finally left work when HR decided to hire Serena after they were convinced that there was more to it than just her looks. Internally I'd rolled my eyes but grinned, they didn't know the half of it. Eventually I'd have to deal with Ceci because I know she's going to be a problem, but for now I don't want to think about her and instead look forward to what this new store and working with Serena will bring. Everything was finally falling into place.

Serena

The last few days I've been in a world of my own, I think it's the shock of seeing Kaleb again. That and the fact I got the job, I'm going to be working under him and I don't know if I can. He's trying to get to me. That interview was utter bullshit. It was just an opportunity for Kaleb to test the waters and try to get under my skin. I tried to keep my cool, and I think I did okay. I didn't give in to him, not like the old me would have.

My heart almost stopped when the other two panelists had left, it turns out that I'd already been shortlisted; they told me that when they invited me to the interview, they just wanted to meet me in person. A face to the name the blonde lady, Carys Ives, had said as she shook my hand, her stern face lit up with a smile. Kaleb grinning at me as he'd pushed my buttons is all I can picture now when I close my eyes. Asking me if I felt anything for him... us, at the end of my interview was a cruel thing for him to do. He left me. I thought my life was going to be smooth sailing, meet a nice guy, buy a house and get married. Things aren't working out like that though, or rather they are but I can't help the small grain of dissatisfaction I feel deep down in my heart.

"I'm going to find some stock cubes— I'll be back in a moment." Sean says as he wanders off down the aisles of our local market. It's Tuesday, the day we do our weekly shop. It's always the same, every week, every Tuesday. *Always the same.* These clockwork habits never bothered me in the beginning, however as I wander around the same aisles, on the same day I fantasize about coming on a Saturday morning. Or heck, even going somewhere else— like the farmers market on a Sunday morning. Or maybe I'd stay in my pajamas and order online from the comfort of my bed?

I pull my coat tighter around me, I just want to curl up and take a few days to sort out my thoughts but I'm never alone. I go home to Sean, I wake up with Sean and then I go to work where Kaleb is in the office preparing for the new opening and it all starts again. There's no space for me right now and I just need to breathe.

I'm busy bagging up some oranges when someone casually bumps against my basket. I look up and go to apologize for being in the way but the words stop in my throat. How does this man always manage to look so damn good? Kaleb's stands before me in another suit perfectly cut to his body, this one a charcoal color. I refuse to believe that it's just a coincidence that he happens to show up at my local market on the one day I'm here. It can't be, can it? But then again what's the other option? My ex-lover has turned into my stalker?

"Hey." He grins at me.

"Evening." I'm brusque; I don't know how to act around him. Lover. Co-worker. Ex-lover. Boss. Love of my life. I'm so confused right now.

"Serena, we didn't get a chance to talk properly the other day." I notice he doesn't have a trolley or a basket with him. Why is he here?

"There's nothing to say Kaleb. I look forward to working with you." I keep my voice calm. I can't let him see how much he gets under my skin.

"That's it?" he looks incredulously at me. Those blue eyes of his are bearing into me and I can feel something inside me beginning to crack. But we can't go there. We can't do this. Kaleb is forbidden territory and heartbreak. I'm going to get burned again if I'm not careful.

I spot Sean down towards the end of the aisles,

he's looking for me. It'll be mere moments before he sees Kaleb and then what? Guilt rises in my throat and makes me feel a little sick; I nod to Kaleb and go to leave, making sure not to touch him as I pass.

He knows I'm avoiding him and his hand flies out to capture mine, he pulls me back to face him. "This is not over, you can keep avoiding me but at some point we're going to have to talk." He reaches up and cups my face, running his thumb over my bottom lip as his eyes pin me in place.

"I am not him, you can't shut me out." He nods towards Sean before removing his hand and leaving the store. My skin burns from where he just touched me and I can feel myself craving more.

I stare down at my shopping basket, my heart racing. I cast my eyes over all the organic vegetables, fruit and quinoa. This is what my life is, healthy and good for you, but ultimately dull. Kaleb is chocolate and wine, and I can't help but keep comparing the two. My mind is a mess and I can't think clearly, it's already started.

"Hey babe, the artichoke is on sale. I was thinking you could make that amazing soup you did for the dinner party the other week." Sean's voice breaks into my thoughts as he stands before me, holding out the artichoke as an offering.

"I'm kind of tired, can't we get takeout? I'll make the soup this weekend." I say weakly, rubbing my forehead.

Sean frowns, "Urm, yeah. Sure." He agrees but I can tell by the sound of the voice he's not happy about it. His latest fad is clean eating and a takeout definitely doesn't come under the clean category yet I can't bring myself to spend all evening cooking. I don't even like artichokes.

KALEB

It was bound to happen sooner or later. I knew I'd have to casually bump into Serena at the supermarket and risk her think I'm stalking her, which I'm not. That wasn't what I was doing at all. Since I'd left her in that hotel room three years ago, I promised myself that I would keep an eye on her and make sure she was taken care of. Definitely *not* stalking.

Many times I had to cover up her boyfriend Sean's mistakes and messes and make sure he was taking care of her. He wasn't though, it wasn't like she hid it well either. Just talking to her for a minute there at the supermarket I could see it all over her pretty face, how unhappy she was. She could go around and tell everyone that she was happy but Serena couldn't hide it from me, I knew her like no other. Sometimes I worried that she was even trying to fool herself.

I had to remind myself that Sean was merely keeping that spot warm for my return and try to push away the jealous thoughts that cropped up every time I thought about them together. He didn't deserve her but I wasn't going to be the one to tell her that. However, I was going to be the one to make her think twice about being with him. Why didn't I tell her what I knew about Sean? I couldn't. There was a part of her that was convinced she still loved him and I couldn't just stomp that out. She had to realize it for herself. She didn't have to know I've been watching out for her all these years. I didn't mean to keep tabs on her; I just never stopped caring about her.

I knew she was the one for me.

That was the reason why I wasn't with Jen anymore. The relationship we had didn't last long after I left because honestly? You just can't force something that isn't there and never really was. But with Serena it was different, and I was going to be around to make her fall for me all over again. I knew she would, it was just a matter of time.

Meanwhile I had to blow off some steam, so I go to the gym and start getting changed into my workout clothes. I catch a sight of the tattoo that I rarely look at. It wasn't the half sleeve on my right arm or the one I got for my grandfather shortly after he passed away about two years ago that was on the right side of my chest. My grandfather, the one I always looked up to next to my dad. It also wasn't the tribal ink I got after leaving this place three years ago on my right leg. No, the tattoo I stared at in the mirror was the simple quote, "Life is too short to wait" written in old English on the right side of my ribs. That tattoo was the most recent and I vividly remembered the day I got it, it was the day I had seen Serena here in town before the company offered me to move me back and start on the new store.

That day had been full of decisions and I got the tattoo because I believed the quote was true. It was also the reason why I was going to fight to get Serena back and this time for good.

Serena

I roll over to see 6:30am flashing angrily at me in the darkness. It's almost time to get up and I've barely slept a wink. Today I'm starting my new job with Kaleb— *with Kaleb*. I keep saying it over and over but it still doesn't feel real. How did we get here? Kaleb, the man who broke my heart is now my boss. I can't seem to stop thinking about him, the way he touched my face and told me we had unfinished business. He looks at me like he wants to devour me, and a small part of me wants him to.

A soft snore beside me interrupts my thoughts. Ever since the market last week Sean has been out of sorts with me. I just assumed he was pouting at me over that stupid soup. He does that a lot recently; he'll shut me out and become distant over the smallest things, sometimes for weeks. It's been getting worse the last couple of years, I guess since the first time Kaleb left. Sean had been getting suspicious, asking me questions about where I was, who I was with and I couldn't take it anymore. I told Kaleb we had to do something, make a choice and he did. He left.

I stayed here and picked up the pieces of my relationship with Sean, it was hard and it doesn't seem to be getting better. He hardly ever touches me these days either, I mean he'll hold my hand, give me a gentle peck on the lips or cuddle me as we fall asleep but there's no spark there anymore. I asked my mother about it once and she briskly shut me down, saying it was normal for couples who'd been together as long as we had. According to her, we just had to make effort with each other. How do you make more effort when you both work full time and have so many other commitments? I try here and there, I dress up, make special dinners and arrange couples weekends away but they're only short term fixes. As soon as we come back home everything goes back to the way it was. I guess the new house adds to the stress. My grandparents left me a nice bit of money in their will, enough for the house deposit and some savings. So we'd taken the next step and bought a house, but it's not perfect and could use some serious improvements. It's something we're working on here and there, but exhaustion and DIY doesn't exactly add to our sex life.

I sigh gently as I look over his sleeping figure, his back turned to me. I miss being wanted. I miss those hungry kisses, the ones where he cups my face and tastes me as if I were the finest champagne. I miss his breath on the back of my neck as his hands slip around my waist and pull me into him. I miss a Sean that no longer exists.

Perhaps never really existed.

I feel a pang of guilt as Kaleb's face flashes into my mind. I stare at the ceiling, trying to banish all thoughts of him, pushing away the memories of stolen nights and feverish kisses. He does something to me that I can't control; I seem to lose my mind around him.

Another glance at the clock tells me I have to get a move on. It's time to face the man I simultaneously fear and want, and I'd better look damn good doing it.

KALEB

I take my coffee to go from the cafe across the street from work. Usually, I take a minute or a few early each morning when the café opens before it gets crowded with people who are also starting their day with a cup of Joe. It's my quiet time before I pour myself completely into work, something that helps me clear my mind and get ready for the day. But today is different.

So I take a sip, burning my tongue but not caring and it has everything to do with the fact a certain someone is about to walk in through the office doors of a place where I spend most of my days. From the minute my eyes opened this morning, my usual regime went out the window. And before my routine kept me focused, it filled my time and gave me a distraction— but now I didn't need it. Today was finally the day when Serena was back in my life. Let operation 'Happily Ever After' begin.

Serena is going to be my diversion now. She has

been the reason or one of the reasons why I had worked well over fifty and sometimes sixty hours per week.

Today is her first day so I make sure to get there early and get everything prepared. I even skip breakfast because I have a plan but that's for later. For now I look over the schedule and make some adjustments. Maybe I'm a little excited but all I know is that I want to spend as much time with her as I can before she goes back home to *him*.

Sean actually called me last night but I ignored it. He didn't leave a message so I didn't think it was important. Either way, I didn't care to speak to him. He saw me at the supermarket but it wasn't really a surprise since he already knew I was back.

Oh yes, I distinctly remembered the last time he called me— before last night— he'd met up with me because he needed money. Of course he did. He was barely able to keep his job and that's only because I talked his boss into giving him another chance. He's lucky that his boss, Tom, is an old acquaintance of mine. I sigh. Why did I let Serena stay with him? He wasn't fucking worthy of her.

Then I remember why and that brings me back to the here and now. So I stop thinking about the one person I hate and start thinking about the person I'm waiting for. It's certainly going to be an interesting day. My master plan is to make her nervous, to play on the fact that I already know she feels something for me. Serena could try to deny our attraction and connection but at the end of the day, I knew she wouldn't. She wouldn't be able to, even if she smacks me for being inappropriate first. I laugh at that thought just as Serena walks through the front door.

My mouth falls open and then closes. She's wearing a black dress that's definitely working for her silhouette. Her hair's up in a bun, minimal makeup but she didn't need it and stilettos that clicked on the floor as she made her way across the office. She looks like a model that has just stepped of the pages a magazine. She's matured since we were last together, and the look works for her.

"Wow," I mutter under my breath.

She looks right ahead but I know she saw me as soon as she walked into the building. Ceci, the training manager, was standing beside me, she hadn't noticed Serena because she was busy talking to the receptionist.

Serena comes to a stop in front of me, now she looks me in the eye as if nothing's wrong, as if there isn't tension between us. I smile kindly and my colleague finally turns around.

"Oh my! Sorry honey, I'm Ceci, your training manager. You'll be working directly with Kaleb which I'm sure you already know. Lucky you!" She winks at me but turns back to look at Serena.

Ceci's the kind of person you could only take so much of. She is a lot to handle and I know because we had a thing once. It just happened after we grabbed some drinks at work one day. That was a mistake I wasn't going to revisit again, no matter how much Ceci pushed the issue. She was a long-legged, thin, blond woman that could probably find someone that would suit her better but she had a crush on me, *a bad one.*

It was somewhat pathetic at times…like now, and it was very unprofessional when she tries to flirt with me in front of other co-workers. Completely ignoring her wink and big smile, I glance back at Serena.

"You're here a little early but I think we're ready for you. If you come with us, we'll start with the tour." Ceci says, not letting my lack of response phase her.

She nods and smiles politely at Ceci but her attention remains on me, "Thank you."

Serena

I feel sick. I knew he was watching me the second I walked through the door, my skin warmed and I knew he was near. My heart began thumping loudly in my chest and I tried to calm myself quickly before he realized what the sight of him did to me. Years later and he was still having this effect on me. I don't think I'll ever be over Kaleb Collins.

A tall skinny blonde lady introduces herself as Ceci and gives me a smile as fake as the color of her hair. Her red talon-like nails gently scratch against my skin and her hand is cold as she quickly shakes mine. The way she eyes me up tells me that there is or was something between her and Kaleb. Typical, does that mean he's fucked everyone on his management team? The jolt of anger I feel scares me a little, because it tells me that I'm jealous. It tells me that I still care. I don't care. I don't.

I'm aware that I'm shaking my head a little, and cover it with a friendly smile. You don't get to work in customer services as long as I have without learning to hold it together when inside you're a mess.

Ceci tells us she's ready for the tour, oozing fake enthusiasm. She'd already decided I am some sort of threat two minutes ago when she winked and I can feel my face tightening in response. I have no time for these childish games; it's hard enough having to be near Kaleb without someone thinking I'm trying to rival them for his attention. Let him have the twig bitch, I just want this job…no matter how delicious he looks in that suit with those tattoos peeking out, inviting me to look. I resist the urge to peel off his shirt and trace my fingers over his body art, instead turning back to Ceci as she gives me a run-down of plans for the day. First up is a tour of the store, then the standard health and safety rubbish, lunch, and then back to the office for contacting suppliers and advertising for new staff. She keeps saying that we need a 'plan of action' and by the fifth time she has said it I want to slap her, but I just nod.

She hands me a hard hat, a neon workers vest and apologizes, telling me that there's been a lighting problem that the construction workers have had to finish last minute. I take them graciously but smile inwardly when I see how the neon vest clashes with her hair.

We head from reception out onto the shop floor, the place is huge and for a moment I forget all about Kaleb and Ceci. Ideas start brewing in my head and I can already see what I think this store needs to make it special and how I'd draw customers in. We walk around the room a few times, discussing displays, budgets and the furniture that's arriving in the next week or so. They want the store open in two weeks and this time my smile is genuine because I know I've got this. Next Ceci and Kaleb give me a tour of the storeroom, which is as large as the storefront, if not slightly bigger. It looks like a warehouse back there, with rows upon rows of shelving and hooks. Again, we traipse up and down amongst the aisles; my feet ache at this point. It was stupid of me to wear my new heels, choosing looks over comfort, I think as I feel the shoes rubbing against the back of my ankles. The raw skin reminds me that I'm letting Kaleb get to me.

I can see him watching me out of the corner of my eye the whole way around. He's dying to say something to me I can see it on his face. Back when we were both just lackeys for this company we wouldn't have hesitated to sneak a cheeky grope or kiss in the storeroom. Now I try to avoid his gaze, because I know he's remembering those embraces just like I am.

Ceci's phone rings loudly, she makes a half-hearted apology about having to take the call and disappears through one of the fire doors. I keep wandering around the stockroom until I hear Kaleb behind me. He's dragged a footstool over from somewhere and plonks it in front of me.

"Sit" he commands, motioning to the stool.

"I'm okay." I say, waving him off. I go to turn away but I feel his hands on my shoulders, he softly pulls me back and pushes me onto the stool. I throw him a look, but the relief on my feet is bliss. He kneels before me and carefully takes a foot in his hand, and cautiously pulls off my stiletto. I make a noise of protest but he silences me by raising his eyebrow at me.

"I saw you hobbling back there. You are not okay."

I just shrug at him. My mouth has gone dry— I don't know what to say. When he's this close to me I can see the flecks of green in his blue eyes. I can see the small scar he has near his bottom lip from a skateboarding accident when he was a kid. I can see the way his mouth crooks when he's displeased with me, especially since he's just seen the state of my blistered feet. I see everything.

I fight the temptation to rest my head on his shoulder and lean into him. I smell the cool minty notes of his aftershave and grimace a little. Here he is fresh, clean cut and handsome holding my blistered foot as I try not to blush. I'm not sure I've ever really been okay since he left, and I don't know what to say or do to change that.

KALEB

The minute Ceci is out of sight, I'm relieved. She's been a real pain in the ass. Although we have to work together, there's only so much I can take of her. Yeah, I may have slept with her but it was never happening again and that was something she just didn't get. Ceci being around Serena worries me because of her attitude. She's been nice enough but it's not real and we all know it. The tension is almost stifling as all the unspoken words hang around us. Still, I couldn't call Ceci out on it and if I do say anything at all, it would only make her happy for acknowledging her in the first place which I'm not about to do.

I'm glad that she took the phone call and left. There was no one that could read Serena's face like me. No one. So when I notice how she's walking and the discomfort on her face tells me everything I need to know. She didn't push me away and she let me take care of her feet, massaging one at a time as she watches me curiously. I let her think I don't notice, instead I stay focused on her soft feet that were being damaged by the new shoes she wore. The thought of her putting herself through such torture made me smile.

"What's that for?" She questions me and I know I'm caught.

I shrug, "Nothing." I don't want to tell her I know why she's gone through the trouble of looking this good and wearing those heels. The moment would be ruined then.

She sighs in relief, "That feels nice." She admits, "But I think that's enough," She tries to pull away but I don't let her.

Holding onto her feet, I put her shoes back on but don't let her go. Instead, my hands work their magic as they slowly make their way up her ankle and then higher.

"Kaleb—" She tries to say, but she's almost out of breath which tells me how much I'm affecting her.

"Hmm?" I say as I look up at her, her eyes half closed as if she's enjoying herself, I know I am.

For a moment I think she's going to push me away but her hand stops mid-air and instead she tentatively touches my shoulder. I know Serena is breaking and it wouldn't be long before I have her completely at my mercy.

"Why are you doing this?" She whispers as I lightly touch her thighs, opening her legs as wide as the dress would allow. She may have looked hot in that outfit but it just wasn't practical for any sexual encounters.

I grin, "Because I know you want it. You want it as much as I do—" My words died in my mouth as I hear familiar heels clicking down the hall.

We both pull away from each other and straighten up. Serena's standing and looking as if nothing had almost happened and I try to do the same. I can see her face shut down as she tries to close me out. Let her try to deny what she feels, when she's in the moment I know that she still wants me.

Ceci gives us a look, "Are we done here? We need to get down to business." Her tone is now bitchy and cold. She didn't wait for an answer before walking away and expecting us to follow. Serena falls in behind her, keeping her eyes trained straight ahead. She looks pissed now and I wonder if she thinks something is going between Ceci and I.

Serena

It was nauseating thinking of Kaleb and Ceci being together, it was an image my jealous heart couldn't handle right now. Ceci had paused when she'd seen us, her reaction a giveaway. She wasn't stupid despite the blonde hair and breezy attitude and I understood the stab of hurt she must of felt. It was the same one I had been feeling all morning.

I didn't allow myself to enjoy Kaleb's hands on me, even if I wanted him. Even if he made my body ache for him, even if I was close to breaking and begging to be touched because I could feel the shame creep in, the guilt gnawing at me all over again. I hated that feeling more than I wanted him. Years ago we had shared a secret and when he left I hoped to bury it. I had hidden it away in a dark corner of my mind, and planned never to bring it back up again. It had been our dirty little secret, our love affair except now it didn't seem like it was. If Ceci could tell just by looking at us for two minutes in a public place, how many other people had known? I wonder how Sean never figured it out? The man who I woke up with every morning, and went to bed with every night had been oblivious and still strangers could tell?

"I think I can take it from here Ceci, you seem to be in a hurry to get back to what you were doing so it's fine. I'll show Serena the ropes; after all she will be working with me mainly." Kaleb announced as we got back to the offices.

Ceci's fake smile was back on her face, "Are you sure? I don't think—"

Kaleb's eyes narrowed as he looked over at her, "It's fine. If I need you, I know where to find you."

Just like that she was dismissed. My eyes widened as she gave me one last look before she turned away and left, her heels click clacking in the distance. Kaleb could be cutting when he wanted to be, management suited him.

"Why were you so rude?" I asked and regretted it the moment the words were out of my mouth. He was my new boss after all.

"Nothing you have to worry about. Come, we have things to discuss." Business man Kaleb was a turn on, I wasn't going to lie. The way he took control and commanded me brought a heat to my cheeks as I imagined him ordering me to strip in the deserted store room. Watching him in that crisp, expensive suit with a grin on his face as I strip away my blouse, peel down my skirt and stand before him in my lacy lingerie. I gave myself a sharp mental slap and try to focus. I follow him back into his office and hope we'll stick to work topics only. Right now my mind was racing just as fast as my heart and I couldn't control my thoughts. I wanted him.

The door shut softly behind us and for some reason I felt like I was trapped. I wished that Ceci had stuck around because with her present nothing could happen. I never thought I'd be using a blonde bimbo as a prevention method against Kaleb.

"So what do you think?"

My throat seemed to have closed up so I tried swallowing before speaking, "About what?"

Kaleb pulled a chair out for me to sit down, his hand resting on the small of my back as he directed me towards it. Shyly I sat, there was something about Kaleb that made me nervous, maybe it was because I knew the destruction, the heat, the passion we were capable of and that frightened me.

"About the store." He said before he went around his desk.

At this point, I knew my panties were soaked. All the sexual tension between us was getting to me and I didn't know what I was going to do about it. I yearned for release, it had been too long since I'd had an orgasm and my body was turning on me. Kaleb cocked his head to the side and waited for my response.

"Yes the store. I've got it."

"How so?" He asked, a small smile forming at the corner of his mouth.

I smiled, "As if you didn't know me. I can already envision it, it's truly going to be amazing when we're done with it."

Kaleb nodded in agreement, "I'm glad you're feeling confident about this Serena. Unfortunately, your office isn't quite finished up, just like everything here. But don't worry, you'll be working in here mostly with me anyway."

"What?" My eyes widened, being in an enclosed space with Kaleb is the last thing I need.

No.

KALEB

"What's wrong?" I ask Serena. Her face paled when I mention that she'll be working in with me. In my book, it's a win, win situation but I didn't like that she wasn't seeing it that way.

She shakes her head, "It's just that— just that, I can't."

"Why?" If there is a real reason, other than the obvious I want to know.

She tries to laugh it off, "There's no space. You have your desk and I—"

"You don't have to worry about it. We can manage. Unless there's another reason as to why you can't work here with me?" I ask coyly. If she's nervous about being close to me I want to hear her say it.

She pauses for a moment, "No but—"

"Then we're good. As I was saying, we have to work on this together and quickly so we get it done in two weeks." I continue, not letting her protests get in the way of my plans.

In the back of my mind I think about taking her in my office as everyone outside goes about their business. Oh yes, this was going to be so good. Serena is a fighter and I know that she's going to try to do whatever she can to stay away from me but she can't. We're like magnets; we'll always find our way back to each other.

Fantasizing about her over my desk had been just that in the past— a fantasy, but now it was something that I knew was going to happen no matter what. Sean be damned, he didn't deserve her. She wouldn't want to go back home to him after work, I'd make sure of it. It was all part of my plan to convince her that I loved her. She'd be so sex addled and addicted to me like before, that when she eventually realized she loved me back it'd be too late. She'd finally be mine. I try my best to keep my face expressionless so she doesn't have any idea about what I'm thinking. I have to move very carefully, this is forever I am playing with.

Throughout the day, I manage to maintain control but not without stealing looks at Serena and a little flirting here and there. What was surprising was that she flirted back and suddenly it was like old times, back when we were both just co-workers at a store. We always had chemistry, from the very beginning when we first set eyes on each other. It was a miracle that no one had suspected anything since our pull towards each other was obvious.

We had changed in the three years that we'd been apart but it wasn't in a way that made us strangers. We were growing as individuals and we were going to find our way back to each other again. Something told me that it would happen sooner rather than later.

Serena

Working so close with Kaleb has me thinking about what I know of love. It has me second guessing what I feel and I don't know how to cope with that. Sean is the man I promised to marry, and I loved him, but there are thoughts that invade my mind when I'm crammed in that office with Kaleb that mess with my head. I try to remember how I met Sean, what he was like and why I fell in love with him but it all becomes so lost, the memories tangled up with what he tells me and what I know now.

Everyone remembers their first kiss. The first time they see the love of their life. The first moment you realize that they had become your whole world and nothing else matters. But with Sean I couldn't. I mean I know we met when I was eighteen, at the coffee shop near his college campus, and I know that he always remembered my order without fail: Mocha Frappuccino with cream and an extra shot of coffee.

However, I can't say that I noticed him until he asked me out and nervously handed me a scrap of paper with his number on. It was then I saw his dark eyes, sandy colored hair and friendly smile. It didn't hit me, this rush of love or lust or whatever it's meant to be. Instead what I had with Sean was slow, creeping up on me over the months we spent together. It was a comfortable love. Safe.

On our first date we went to the movies, I can't remember what we saw but I remember laughing so hard my sides hurt. I remember the warmth of his skin as he took my hand in his own and I felt nervous: was he going to kiss me? He didn't. He waited until we'd been on four dates before he leaned in and touched his lips to mine. There were no sparks, but then again I'd been raised to know that sparks and fireworks were fantasy, and that real love wasn't anything like that.

Except now I know different.

I know that I keep comparing Sean to Kaleb, and somewhere in the back of my mind I know that's not fair, but I can't help it. What I feel when I'm with Kaleb is like standing in the burning sunshine, your skin on fire while your throat desperately tries to suck in cool air so that you can breathe. Then there's Sean, who is as steady and constant as the rain in Wales.

Your socks squelch inside your soaked shoes, and you're cold but you know that's just how it is and there's nothing you can do about it.

My mother took to Sean straightaway, commenting on how charming he was and how my Grandmother back in Cardiff would be so happy I'd found someone so reliable. There was this instant pressure for me to be the perfect girlfriend for him, the perfect fiancé and I would be expected to be the perfect wife too no doubt. I loved my family, but at times they could be too overbearing, trying to convince me that what they wanted for me is what I should want too and sometimes it just doesn't work like that. Sean's mother was just as bad as mine, the two in cahoots since the day we made our relationship official. They'd begun picking out engagement rings, baby names, who would get Thanksgiving and who would get Christmas and this was all before we'd even moved in together. My life, this big, huge thing of endless possibilities suddenly closed in around me, like a hermit crab retreating into its shell. And I thought I was okay with that, but every day that passes I know that I'm not and a small part of me is itching to climb outside this life that traps me. Kaleb is just my catalyst, and three years ago I was ready to make that move, to leave my 'perfect life' behind for him but he said we had to end it. That we couldn't keep hurting Sean and Jen, his girlfriend at the time and I felt that he couldn't love me the way I loved him. It hurt. It really fucking hurt, but it made me want to give Sean another chance, to see if I was just over reaching for things I couldn't have with Kaleb. Then the weeks of trying turned into months, and then years. Before I knew it I was eating clean food, cooking artichokes and buying a house with yellow wallpaper.

And now I'm working for my ex-lover, the man I had an affair with. I'm employed by the man who put my steady life in jeopardy with his sexy smile and his sinful eyes. I feel like sometimes I have to pinch myself, as if none of this is real.

But here I am, sitting at my desk, which mirrors his in this tiny little room so we're facing each other all day, every day. Well, it isn't tiny but with both of our desks and various filing cabinets there's limited space. He makes jokes, gives me one of those secret smiles here and there and I feel myself relaxing around him. I even start flirting back a little— it's dangerous territory.

KALEB

She's watching me, I can feel her eyes on me as I type away on the keyboard and try to focus on what I'm doing. Serena's working too but she can't hide the glances she steals when I'm not looking and I don't call her out on it either. Something like calmness comes over me and it's nice for once to feel like someone actually cares about me. Although Jen *cared* about me at some point, we never had the kind of chemistry that Serena and I did, it wasn't like this.

I don't know how I got through the last 3 years without being able to see, talk to or touch Serena. Now that she's back in my life, I couldn't imagine leaving. *Never again.* I decide that I can't and won't leave her. Sean may have been what she wanted years ago and maybe she wanted to have that happily ever after with him, but then...maybe not. It wasn't like she ever actually told me she chose him, she didn't. I just thought that's what she wanted because we never talked about how we felt about each other. I feel a surge of jealously go through me whenever I think of Sean. I hate that fucker.

We both knew that we couldn't have a relationship without hurting others in the process. We used that as an excuse to end our affair, but now I knew better and it wasn't completely about Jen or Sean, we just weren't prepared to deal with the consequences at the time.

Now?

Now I know that Sean never changed and never will. Now I know that Serena missed me just as much as I had missed her. The way she looks at me and how I've seen her react to my closeness and my touch tells me everything, even if she tries to deny it. We're about done for the day but I just can't let her go without addressing this build-up of sexual tension that's killing me. I shut my laptop down and straighten out some paperwork as Serena is getting her purse, she's about to leave too.

"Productive day wasn't it?" I comment as I walk around my desk towards hers.

Serena is about to walk out the door but she turns and smiles, "It was. We got lots done ready for the opening. Tomorrow is going to be super busy as well, so see—"

I come closer, "In a hurry?" I cut her off before

she says good bye. Now I wonder if I hadn't said anything if she would've even acknowledge my presence before walking out the door. Her face tells me that yes she didn't want to have this conversation.

"I just— I need to—" She tries to say but she's looking away now and I know she's trying to come up with an excuse for why she's suddenly so desperate to leave.

Now her back is against the door and I'm a few inches away, "Shh," I touch her lip lightly with a finger and tuck a lock of a stray hair behind her ear, "Am I making you nervous?" I want to know.

She starts to shake her head but I lift her chin up so she looks me in the eye and she nods instead. I can tell she *is* nervous and that excites me. I'm grinning now but she doesn't like it and tries to turn and open the door but I put hand over the door to keep her from leaving.

"Not so fast, you know you feel this tension too and I know you want me Serena, you know you do." I know it even if she doesn't admit it. I press my body against her back and she gasps in surprise. She doesn't move and it's as if I could hear both our hearts beating fast. She's trying to control her breathing but I smile inside, knowing her all too well.

"Tell me, does *he* make you feel this way?" The

words come out and it's not what I intended to say but it's out there nonetheless, so I own it. My envy creeping out. She's going home to *him*. I almost touch her but I hold back because I want to know.

She looks over her shoulder, "Kaleb. Please stop." Her voice is even and firm which makes me pause.

We stare at each other for what seems like eternity but I don't want to push too hard, I just want her to know that I'm here and I'm not going anywhere. I want her to feel it, feel me and I know that Sean can't compare.

"Fine, but you know he doesn't. *Sweet dreams Serena.*" I whisper close to her ear and step away.

She darts out of the office without a word or even looking back at me. It wasn't my intention to make her nervous exactly but my jealousy took over. It also served to prove my point further and now I know for sure that soon she'll be begging for me *not* to stop.

Serena

I'm out of the office all morning the next day, meeting with suppliers and interviewing the final recruitments. Everything is finally falling into place and we're almost set to open up the store.

I sneak off to lunch at a local diner without stopping to check in with Kaleb or any of the staff milling about. I don't want him trying to join me because I need some time to get my thoughts together, and out of the gutter. Last night I dreamed about him, *about us*. I dreamt of the weekend we spent tucked away on the outskirts of town in a small boutique hotel. It was a haze of sunlight streaming in the windows, laughter and him, our bodies touching, being connected in a way that I'd never felt before. Flashes of skin, the feel of his kisses, soft caresses and the weight of his body covering mine. I hadn't wanted to wake up and when I did I was sweating, with an ache in my chest that I couldn't name right now. I was also hornier than I'd been in a while, something that was making me blush every time I thought about Kaleb – let alone if I had to sit opposite him for hours.

I check my watch and realize my lunch break is over and I'm no closer to regaining my composure. I'd better just face him head on and make sure that I'm firm with my boundaries. Sean isn't helping my resolve, this morning before I left for work he hadn't said a word to me, and that was after he crawled into bed last night reeking of booze. The smell coming off him as he fell into a deep sleep was enough to make me gag. I can feel my respect for him slipping away, these days everything he does seems to grate on me and I have to bite my tongue.

Looking up I see 'our' office, the walk from the diner back to work a blur as I was lost in my thoughts, trying to untangle my feelings. My heart stops as the door swings open and Kaleb looks furious, and sexy— always sexy.

"Get in here." He demands and like a meek little sheep I do.

He closes the door with more force than necessary. He's angry with me. He knows I've been avoiding him.

Kaleb backs me up against the wall, there's a gleam in his eyes that scares me. That fear sets my body on edge and I can feel everything. I feel his hot breath as it tickles my neck, gently blowing some of my lose hair across my skin as he inhales and exhales steadily. His hand twitches down by my hip, his fingertips barely brushing against me and I know he's itching to touch me. A shiver runs through me. I know I'm already lost to him and that scares me – but that doesn't mean I have to make it easy on him.

For a moment, we're stuck, staring at each other with our gazes locked – I say nothing, I give him nothing. I want him and he knows it, that's why he's playing with me but I refuse to say the words. I refuse to give him permission to take what's always been his.

"Where the fuck have you been?" His voice is gravelly and low, like he's been shouting all morning, which he probably has. When Kaleb is annoyed, there's no containing his wrath. This man is all about expressing himself, he knows who he is and he doesn't shy away from it.

He places his hands on either side of me, pinning me in place and I tilt my face up to his, showing my defiance in the only way I feel brave enough to do.

"I had meetings and then I was at lunch. I was doing what you pay me to do— *work*."

His green eyes narrow at me and finally, hoarsely he asks "Were you with Sean?"

He's jealous. He thinks I was with Sean on my

break, and I want to reassure him, tell him that I wasn't. But it's nothing to do with him. I let out a soft sigh, sooner or later he'll realize he's crossing a line but right now he's like a bull with a red flag.

"It's nothing to do with you." I reply gently.

"You *are* mine. Always mine." He growls and another shiver runs through me. I wish I was, but I'm not.

I turn my face away from him, before I say something stupid like 'Yes please!' because Kaleb gets under my skin like no one else. My body longs for his touch, and I want nothing more than to grab his face and kiss him like there's no tomorrow— but boundaries. I have to have boundaries. I should stop this before it gets started.

His hand comes under my chin and he pulls me to face him, his lips are on mine before I can stop him. His tongue finds mine; he tastes of mint with a hint of coffee, all things Kaleb. His body presses into mine, and I want to melt into him, and for him to devour me. Three years we'd been apart. Three years too long was all I could think as his hands grab my wrists and pin them above my head. His thigh snakes between my legs, rubbing against me and I let out an involuntary gasp. One of his hand snakes down my body and reaches for the hem of my skirt and suddenly I panic.

I can't do this. I'm getting married. I won't go back to being his bit on the side that he dumps when he gets bored. I pull myself free of his grip, bring my hands down to his chest and push him away firmly.

"I am *not* yours Kaleb, I never was." And before I register what I'm doing I slap him across the face. The crack of my hand meeting his skin has us both shocked and breathing heavily he grabs his suit jacket and leaves, slamming the door behind him. He comes back an hour later but he doesn't say a word for the rest of the day.

KALEB

Serena just left the office.

We had stayed behind late after our argument to work and yes, it was actually work, thanks to her rejection. *She. Rejected. Me.* I'm still trying to process what went down since it all happened so fast. I want her, every single inch of her but I want her to come willingly. I need her to love me the way she used to. I didn't think she would reject me, I thought she was ready but obviously not. I let my temper get a hold of me, my jealousy causing me to lash out. I had a plan in place to win her back but when I'm around her it all goes to hell.

"Fuck." I say out loud as I re-read the document I've been holding in my hand for the past ten minutes. I've never been rejected like that before; Serena pushed me and slapped me?I couldn't believe it. She was like a new person but not really, back when she was mine she started coming out of her shell. She'd always had that feistiness within her but the only time I ever really got a glimpse of it was between the sheets. Sooner or later she wouldn't be able to refuse me again. I just knew she wouldn't. Deep down, she *still* loved me. I felt it. She was mine because she'd claimed a part of my soul two years ago, my heart was hers and I had to show her that. I needed to keep a cool head and win her back, they say lust is only temporary but I was going to use it to reel her in.

The rest of the afternoon dragged by and you could tell we were both tense. We avoided small talk and focused on work right up until it was time to clock out. I watched her gather up her coat and bag, never forgetting that she has someone waiting at home. That thought pisses me off more, on top of everything else. It was the reason I took my anger out on half the staff while she was gone earlier. The thought of her still being with Sean made me sick. To distract myself I decide to stay on and work. I don't want to do something drastic, like try and stop her from getting in her car or following her home. The jealousy is driving me so crazy right now that I wouldn't put it past me, but I had to hang back—just a little longer.

As I start to shut everything down, there's a knock

at the door. Who could be here so late? I was sure everyone had left a while ago.

I answer and regret it the minute I open the door.

"Of course you'd still be here." Sean says as he pushes his way inside the office leaving the stench of alcohol trailing behind him, I make a face and turn to watch him. What the fuck is he playing at? He's disoriented but he tries to look cool as he walks around my office.

"Why are you here?" I ask exasperated. I don't want deal with his bullshit tonight.

He laughs, "Why do you think big shot?" He turns to glare at me, "I knew you'd be back one day and I knew you'd want to take her from me. I'm here to tell you you're wasting your time. She wants to be with me—" He starts to raise his voice.

"Oh for fuck sake Sean!" I hiss, if I was pissed off earlier, now I'm beyond furious, "If it wasn't for me she would never have stayed with you and that's a fact."

That fucking idiot has some balls walking into my office drunk and claiming Serena like she was a piece of property. I sound like a hypocrite but there's a difference between what he has with Serena and what I've always had with her. Sean never respected her in any aspect and we both know it, but she doesn't. How does that saying go? Ignorance is bliss and all that? A part of me wished that she could see him for who he truly is, and what I'd give to make her happy. I loved her so much I'd only left to give us both a shot. That had been a mistake but once she found out the truth, she'd know what a real piece of shit he was. Serena's happiness was built upon a foundation made of sand, and one day she'd see the monster he really was. Not that she would think I'm a saint in all this. I knew that if we had a relationship— a *real* relationship that is— it wouldn't be like what she has with Sean. Everything I ever did was to protect her and because I thought she truly wanted him. Even if I made a mistake to walk out of her life before, I wouldn't do that again. I wasn't Sean and I was prepared to spend the rest of our lives proving that to her.

Sean stumbles as he shambles towards me but regains his balance quickly.

"Maybe. I guess we'll never find out now will we?" He chuckles, "Even if she does end up sleeping with you again, she's still coming home to me. Every. Night."

He has a point and that makes my blood boil. I couldn't show my hand to him— not yet. "You're out of your fucking mind coming here. All I ever wanted was for Serena to be happy and I know she isn't. She'll never burn for you like she does for me. I give her the confidence to light up the fucking room while you tear her down." I never told him that before but it's true.

Sean tries to charge at me but I move out of the way and he trips then falls down on his own.

"Look at you." I spit, "You haven't changed. I don't know why I even bother trying to help. Every time I do, you just turn right around and fuck everything up again." It was the God's honest truth and I didn't know how Serena could be so clueless.

Sean grins and stands up. "Because," he points at me, "you wouldn't have a chance with Serena if she knew that you helped me. You knew and never said a word. You knew about the gambling and me taking her savings, and the worst part? You knew about the women."

"Get out. Get the fuck out before I do something I won't regret." I say through gritted teeth.

It's a warning and even though Sean's drunk, he knows enough to understand that I'm dead serious. I'd bet my life that Serena is probably at home sleeping, unaware of what was going on, of what her dirty rat of a fiancé gets up to on her dime. I didn't know how she was oblivious to him stumbling around the house in his condition and just throw him out.

Sean glares at me but leaves without saying another word. It's in his best interest to keep silent since I'm the only one who knows his secret. I'm the one that has helped him cover it up this entire time. It's a funny thing how it all comes back into a full circle. The money Sean took out of Serena's account now was mine since I'd kept replacing it for him. He knows this and is threatened by me and that makes me feel like I had the upper hand in this situation but only for a second. His words destroy that train of thought, bringing my plans crashing down.

If Serena finds out about everything, I didn't think she'd ever forgive me. She'd see me as she would see Sean and I couldn't do it. It may be selfish but now that I have her back in my life, I wanted to keep her there. I'd have to find a way for Sean to want to get out of the picture all by himself so she could finally move on.

The question is, how?

Serena

Sean came in drunk again.

I rolled over when I heard him struggling with his key in the door and pretended to be asleep. I can't cope with his drama right now, but it seems like he doesn't want to give me that choice as he barges into the room and tears the blanket off me. As the cold air hits my body I'm shocked and pissed off. Between Kaleb trying to claim me as his today, and Sean treating me like the shit on his shoe lately my head is fried.

"What are you doing!" I shout, sitting up to look at him with my strappy nighty barely covering my body, I start to shiver.

His face is dark, angry as he stands there clutching the duvet to him like he's mad at it. He's practically shaking. "You're pushing me away..." he spits out, slurring and wobbling on his feet.

"No, I'm not," I tell him calmly. "You're drunk Sean. Take off your jeans and get into bed."

"No." He grumbles.

"Fine, then at least give the blanket back."

He throws it at me and glares, his eyes raking over my half naked body and I feel sick. He comes close and sits on the edge of the bed, leaning in towards me. I place a hand on his shoulder, not only to steady him but to also stop him from trying to kiss me because I think that's what he's trying to do.

He puts his hand over mine, and pulls it up to his lips where he gently kisses my knuckles. He rubs his face over my hand, his stubble scratching me, whispering something over and over again. I can't quite make it out, but it almost sounds like he's saying 'sorry'.

Then he lunges for me, like I knew he would. His lips smash against my face, and he practically head butts me as he's misjudged the distance. I push him away gently, as his greedy hands start pulling at my clothes. I can feel the wetness of his mouth on my shoulders and my neck as he grips me tighter to him. I push harder, but his drunken mind isn't getting the message.

Finally I give him a sharp shove and firmly tell him 'No'. He looks at me like it was him I slapped and not Kaleb. Then his hurt distorts into rage, and I feel genuinely afraid. My heart begins to beat faster, louder, and my breath catches.

"You frigid bitch!" He screams at me, droplets of spit hitting my cheek as I try to turn away from him.

He stands unsteadily and looms over me, his hand is raised as if he wants to slap me but he doesn't. He never would. At least the old Sean never would, this version of Sean becomes a stranger to me more and more each day. He stumbles from the room, moments later the front door shuts and the house settles into an eerie quiet, the atmosphere charged with fear and anger. I try to sleep but I can't, so instead I just toss and turn until my alarm goes off at 6:30am.

I pour myself a strong cup of coffee the second I get into work, I take the steaming mug into the office and I plan to apologize to Kaleb for yesterday. I let things go too far, I didn't set out my boundaries and instead I let him kiss me. I wanted him to. Kaleb is my own brand of heroin, addictive but deadly.

I feel like shit, I'm tired and Sean's erratic behavior is playing on my mind. Sean has always been loving and caring, so perfect, almost too perfect. Lately things have been off kilter but there are still days when he's his normal charming self, like last week he brought me home a bunch of tulips for no other reason than it was a Tuesday. I think that's why

I keep holding on, it's why I stay. Well, that and the guilt. It seems silly but I feel like I owe Sean. I feel like I have to keep holding on to this relationship and reviving it because he loves me, and I cheated.

I broke us, and I'm trying desperately to fix us but I'm so tired, so worn down. My heart is heavy and I feel like I'm carrying the weight of us on my shoulders. I'm lost in thoughts of my fragile relationship when Kaleb strides in; his face softens when he sees me. I expect him to be angry with me, annoyed at least, but nothing prepares me for the embrace he pulls me into.

He places his large, strong hands on my shoulders and pulls me into the safe haven of his arms. My cheek rests against his chest and I can hear the steady beating of his heart. I feel safe. I feel loved. I can't stop the tear that starts to trickle down my cheek, its wetness reminding me of how broken everything is.

He squeezes me tighter, and I wish that he would envelop me. I take a deep breath and look up at him and he strokes my hair silently, comforting me in the only way he can. Yesterday's incident is forgotten.

I realize that in this moment I want nothing more than to kiss him, to feel his lips on mine. To be connected, however briefly. I stand on my tiptoes and press my mouth to his. He takes up on my signal without hesitation. His arms snake around my waist, pulling me closer— if that was even possible. His tongue meets mine, and our kiss is not rushed or frenzied but slow, sweet and consuming. It's a slow burn, working its way through my limbs to wash away all the stress, pushing each negative thought away until there is only him.

This time he is the one who ends it, gently pulling away with a sad look on his face. "Not like this." He says as he strokes my cheek.

KALEB

I thought work would be fun having Serena around.

Well I was wrong.

It was fucking torture and to make matters worse we kissed again…Now I can't stop thinking about it and especially how she reacts to my touch and how she leans into me further as I pull her in— damn.

It happens every time I'm near her, I find myself in the moment forgetting about everything and everyone, there is only Serena. She wasn't happy with Sean and I don't know why Serena didn't just end the relationship. I can see the misery in her eyes, she looks tired, worn down and I hate seeing her that way. I hate Sean for what he does to her. It makes me angry to think that I can give her all she's ever wanted but she has to see that for herself. I must prove it to her, but he's in my way.

I made a promise to myself before I came back that things would be different. That I'd find a way to make amends for leaving Serena, that she would finally be happy with me and that we weren't going to fall back into what we had before. So I can't stand how sad she is as she kisses me.

The feeling was too familiar, too much of the past haunted us and I didn't want that looming over us forever. When we had started messing around years ago, it was supposed to be just physical. Even though we tried to keep it that way we couldn't stop the lines blurring. Now, I don't want it to just be physical, I want her completely. I want her heart to be mine and I don't care how selfish that is.

It's why I walk away, it reminds me of the old us and that's not how it's going to be, not again. Although the kiss is sweet, it's not like the others we've shared and it's not fair to either one of us to pretend it's anything more than her being upset with Sean. No, I can't do it that way.

If she's going to be mine, it's going to be because she wants me, because *I* make her blush every time I touch her and get so close— not because she has a grudge against *him* or whatever this is, I just know this kiss is not about me. It's about him. He's everywhere. I fucking hate him. I hate how he sleeps beside her, how he makes breakfast next to her each morning. My hands curl into fists when I think of how little he cares about her and she still goes home to him to their perfect picket fenced house every day.

Am I going to be the one she uses to forget about Sean? Yes, but she has to have feelings for me, she has to want me in the way I need her. Right now I think a part of her still loves him, just because they've been together for so long, she doesn't know any other kind of love. His shrewd and fucked up "love"— if it is even that— isn't enough because if it was then she wouldn't be so sad. She wouldn't have tried kissing me like that, it wasn't meant for me.

I see the look in her eyes before I walk away and it kills me. It's not easy to turn away from the person you love. It's just— she's emotional, I get that but I want her to understand that there's no room for three people in this relationship; it should be just me and her, not me, her and *Sean*.

I grit my teeth as I take a walk to the café where I stop by in the mornings, I need some alone time to clear my head. Maybe it's my fault she's feeling this way too, I'd been pushing her pretty hard at work and then she goes home to *him*. I don't know what happens there. We don't talk about it but I have a vague idea. It's definitely not a fairy tale and even though I'm a hundred percent sure he's not prince charming, I won't be the one to tell her that even though I could.

I order an iced vanilla coffee, watch people go about their lives like bees busy in a hive and I plot. I have to think about what will happen next. Waiting for her to come to me isn't working as well as I'd hoped. She's misplacing her emotions, but she has to want me, not use me as a comfort blanket. Serena has to realize that I could offer her everything, lust, love, friendship and a place to feel safe. But first she had to choose me. Sean needed to fuck off and it was time I upped my game. I couldn't take many more nights thinking of his slimy hands all over her body. If she wasn't going to come straight out and admit how much she wanted me for me, then I'd make her so horny that she'd be begging for me instead. It was time for a more aggressive approach.

Serena

I've been walking around work with my head down ashamed that Kaleb had rejected my kiss a few days ago, but also that I'd even tried. I was engaged, and at some point I'd be marrying Sean— I couldn't act like this. It was getting easier to pretend that nothing had happened as work got busier though, there were new office members, storeroom staff had been hired and I'd just finished going through my pile of 'maybes' for cashiers. I was on a roll and totally in my element, after all I'd started as a cashier myself and worked my way up so I knew the ins and outs of this job.

I barely register Kaleb as he sweeps past me; I was too focused on the new contracts that needed redrafting before they got sent out. But boy do I notice when he grabs me by the elbow, spins me back in the direction I'd just come from and hustles me inside a nearby storage cupboard.

"What do you think you're playing at?" I grind

out indignantly as he locks us in the small space. I'm busy and I don't have time for a closet rendezvous— not that this was what it was. We were past all of that. He rejected me and that stung.

"Me? You're the one who slapped me and then kisses me a day later!" He's standing so close to me I can feel the tips of his toes flush with mine. He places one hand against a shelf behind my head and the other softly strokes my cheek. I know Kaleb like I know my own skin, he's worried about me but there's also something else tinged in his gaze— he wants me. He stares at me like I'm a helpless sheep caught in his wolfish clutches. I bite my bottom lip, trying to avoid looking into his eyes because he'll only see mirrored in them the lust I also can't hide.

"I— I was, there was a lot going on okay?" I fiddle with the file down by my side as Kaleb slips a hand under my chin and forces me to look at him. His blue eyes are stormy, flecks of grey breaking up the swirls of blue and I'm getting lost in them as he refuses to break eye contact.

"No, it's not okay. You see this mouth," he runs a thumb across my bottom lip, "This mouth is mine."

He doesn't kiss me, just continues swiping his thumb roughly across my lip but I feel excitement bubble up within me. His hand trails down my neck,

I can feel the calloused skin as his fingers wrap around my throat.

"See this pretty little neck? That's mine too." He growls as he leans in and nips the sensitive skin. He unbuttons the top of my blouse and cups my breasts through the fabric, laying lingering kisses on my cleavage. "Mine" he mutters between each one and I want to pull him closer to me but I can't because then he'll stop what he's doing.

I sigh quietly and he takes that as a sign to cup my ass and grind me against him, whispering 'Mine' over and over again. The file slip from my grip, sheets of paper sliding across the floor. He grabs my legs, lifts me and without thinking I wrap them around his waist. My skirt is now bunched up around the tops of my thighs and I can feel his erection pressed against my lace panties. I want this. I want him.

One hand comes back up to my face while the other holds me up by grabbing my ass, and he kisses me, my face cupped like I was water, giving life to a thirsty man. It's like we were never apart, like the affair never ended, and I'm lost in the taste and the touch of him. I'm coming apart in his hands just like I always do and while it scares me, it also feels like the most natural thing in the world.

Last time he tried to claim me, I denied I was his,

we both knew I was lying and when the word 'Yes' leaves my mouth I do nothing to try and stop it. I've always been his.

He freezes as we hear someone turn the door handle and walk away, growling again he drops me back to my feet and helps me button up my blouse. He smooths my skirt down, carefully brushing away the dust that I picked up off the shelves behind me. His actions are loving, considerate and opposite to the caveman treatment I was getting a few moments ago.

"This isn't finished." He said, his voice low and gruff as he disappears back out into the corridor.

KALEB

Damn. I can't stop thinking about what happened earlier, the way she practically melted into me. Her tits, her ass— all mine, except they weren't but soon they would be. I didn't mean to be quite so rough, so direct with her but fuck; when I'd seen her walking down the corridor with her mouth turned down I had to do something. When I pulled her into that closet I didn't have a clue what I was doing, but being that close to her drove me wild and I just went with it. I'm glad I did too, my woman lit up like the Eiffel tower. If someone hadn't tried interrupting us I'd have gone further. It seems that Serena wants me, but she doesn't want to say it, which is fine. For now.

Now we're in a meeting with the district manager and we are sitting next to each other. As the presentation starts, the lights are turned off and everyone is facing the front of the room. We are the first to watch a new video that the new employees would have to see during orientation. The hard part is sitting so close to her and not being able to touch her again. I want to do more than just kiss her.

The way her skirt slides up her thighs as she makes any kind of movement on her chair, it's almost as if it was calling my name. She twirls her hair and if I didn't know any better, I'd swear she's playing with me. It's as if she knows she has my complete attention.

I have to keep up my poker face, if not for my own pride at least out of respect for everyone in the room. They don't need to know the dirty thoughts I have about the woman sitting so close to me, I could touch her right now without anyone noticing.

Yes...in fact, that's brilliant! I told her that we weren't finished and I meant it.

Everyone's attention is on the screen at the front of the room. Some lady was going on about safety procedures, blah, blah, blah. I honestly stopped listening five minutes into the boring training video, I felt sorry for the new employees that would have to sit through it and pay attention in order to answer some test questions at the end of it. Serena seemed to be paying attention to it as well but something told me she wasn't actually as into it as our co-workers were.

Maybe it was in the way she was acting, the way she moved restlessly on the chair or her inability to keep her legs still underneath the table. The placement of her hands... Those little things I had come to learn about her. She may believe that she was different this time around, but I still know how she thinks, how her body works. Slowly I place my hand on her thigh, pushing her skirt up in a slow movement under the table.

Serena straightens up, her hand moving on top of mine as if to stop me. I glance at her to give her a look and she pulls her hand away immediately. Good girl, I want to tell her. She wants this just as badly as I do.

Her skin's smooth and all I want is to be between those legs. There's something hot about doing something you shouldn't be, especially in public where you could easily be caught. I've always been a daredevil, just ask my family, even now that I'm older, I still liked to take risks. The only risk I regret is the one I didn't take with Serena years ago. I won't make that mistake again.

She wants to push me away, I know, but that's part of the fun. As the video goes on, I've managed to move my hand up higher until I can feel the warmth of her pussy near my fingers.

So close.

Serena struggles to control her breathing as I touch her through her panties. Her hand is covering her mouth now as she tries to act nonchalant, like she's interested in the safety talk, but she's trying to hide the fact that she's biting down on that sexy bottom lip. I pause to look around the room and make sure no one has noticed anything out of the ordinary— they haven't. We've been lucky to have the back seats so it's just us and unless someone looks underneath the table, they won't be able to see a thing.

Her panties are soaked. *Fuck.*

It's going to be a bitch to get this boner to go down before we have to go back to work. Regardless, I touch her through the wet damp underwear, swirling my finger over the fabric in slow, lazy circles. Serena's head now rests on her hands as she pretends to be engrossed on the training video. I know better though, she's barely keeping it together and honestly, so am I. At least I'm the one giving the pleasure; if the roles were reversed I'm not sure I could stay outwardly as calm as she is. In fact I'm pretty sure I'd be fucking her on the desk— job be damned. Let them watch.

I have the urge to pull her panties aside and slide

my finger inside her wetness but instead I continue with the same motion until her legs close and her thighs stop my wandering hand.

She's close already, and I grin as I pull my hand away slowly. Serena doesn't look at me, she keeps her eyes trained on the screen but I can see the relief on her face. She almost came in front of everyone and I know she isn't always on the quiet side. It's one of my favorite things— making her scream in pleasure.

Shit, I almost embarrassed us both in a room with other co-workers. It's driving me crazy though, being around people and not being able to touch her. I'd had several cold showers a day since she started working with me and they weren't exactly working. The lights flicker on and I stay seated waiting for my hard on to go away. Everyone stands and filters out except Marshall, Serena and an assistant who's collecting up her notes.

"Kaleb are we going to have everything in order for the new employees?" Marshall asks looking at me with a bored look on his face. Glad to see I wasn't the only one.

"Yes sir." I respond, "Everything is still on schedule."

"Very good. Serena how are you finding work? Is Kaleb treating you well?" His question catches me off guard mainly because as far as I'm aware, he doesn't know about our history together.

Serena smiles, "Great, it's been challenging but Kaleb has been very hands on." It's all she says but it's enough for Marshall to move onto the other staff, missing the dig she just had at me.

"Mary, how are the Christmas party preparations going?" He asks the lady who stayed behind as Ceci enters the room.

"Not bad, I have almost everything organized." She doesn't sound too sure but she's one of the more capable assistants so I know she'll get it done.

"Christmas party?" Serena looks at me for an answer.

"Right!" Ceci says, overhearing, "You weren't here before so you don't know."

No shit, she's pointing out the obvious but no one pays any attention to her.

"Next weekend is our Christmas party. It's not a big deal but we do like to get into the spirit of the holidays." Mary replies, smiling at Serena.

"Yes, we're glad you're here for it." I say grinning.

Marshall stands to leave, "Great, let's get together after the Christmas party to see how everything is progressing."

Serena

Yesterday was intense. Kaleb had been taunting me, teasing me in front of everyone— and I loved it. I had to clamp my legs shut tight on his hand to stop myself from coming. This game we were playing was getting riskier, hotter and hornier every step of the way. I just wasn't sure how long I could play along for.

As I pour myself a cup of tea I notice a new sheet on the staffroom communications board and before I even read it, I know what it is. The crappy clipart presents along the bottom and the Christmas tree on the top left hand corner tells me that it's the Christmas party sign-up sheet that Ceci had been talking about. In retail we celebrate Christmas either earlier in November, or later in January because getting time off in December is manic. Plus it's our busiest period. People start coming into the staff room and excitedly scrawling their names down.

"Are you going?" A voice to my right asks, I turn and see Sharon looking at the sheet.

I can see Kaleb's name written neatly at the top and I think about how going to the work Christmas party is just asking for trouble. We've been playing with fire in the office, but combine that with alcohol, dark corners and revelry, I'm just asking to be burned.

"I don't think so…" I reply quietly, taking another gulp of my tea. It burns in my chest that Ceci's name is written below his in her flowery script.

She laughs, "Afraid you'll drink one too many and try to get naked with me in the copy room?"

I say smiling at her, "You're not my type."

She scoffs "Ohhhh yeah, that's because you only have eyes for Mr-Tall-Dark and Sexy."

"W-w-what?" I stare at her, Sharon is one of the new admin staff for the main office but she sees far too much. I knew she was perceptive when I met her, I just didn't realize how switched on she was.

"Everyone knows it Serena. It's just one of those things." She shrugs and wanders over to the counter to pour herself a cup of coffee.

"One of what things? Sharon— what the heck are you on about?"

"The harder you hide it, the more obvious it

becomes. Just sayin'." She calls out over her shoulder as she leaves the staffroom.

I hide my blush by looking down until I get to our office. Mine still isn't finished, and if I didn't know any better I'd say that Kaleb was purposely delaying its completion.

He's in there waiting for me, watching me like always. He rises as I enter and shuts the door behind me, his body almost pressed up against mine. I hate how small this office is sometimes, and at others…I bite my lip. I can smell his cologne mixed with the gentle mint from his toothpaste and I want to kiss him, bury my face in his neck and inhale everything that is Kaleb Collins. I place a hand on his chest, trying to keep a safe distance between us.

"We can't." I whisper. Be firm I tell myself.

He reaches out and tucks a stray strand of hair behind my ear, his fingertips just grazing me, "You keep saying that Serena, and yet here we are."

"It's wrong Kaleb and you know it." I don't look away because I can't, his gaze holds me firmly in place.

"When something feels this good, this right…" He says, placing a gentle kiss on my neck, "How can you say it's wrong?"

I let out a soft moan as the warmth of his lips

makes me shiver, "Because we're hurting people." "Who?" He asks before scraping his teeth softly over the sensitive skin at the curve of my neck. His hand has slid down to my hip and he pulls me into him. Being wrapped up with Kaleb is like coming home. I feel safe, wanted and needed. I can feel how much he wants me through the thin cotton of my skirt and that only serves to push at my resolve.

"Sean. Jen. You know…the people we love." I rasp out as his teeth catch my earlobe before he sucks at it, teasing me.

"You don't love him. As for Jen and I, we were over a long time ago."

KALEB

Serena mentions Jen and I want to laugh because there hasn't been anything between Jen and me for a long time, even when I was still with her. In fact, I stopped having any kind of feelings for her as soon as I realized what Serena meant to me. It hasn't always been that way though. Our relationship had changed dramatically since we finished school.

When I first met Jen, it was over five years ago and since then, we both grew and changed. We were just finishing college and it was the first serious relationship for either of us and I thought it was perfect. She was the social butterfly, she was smart and funny. Effortlessly charming compared to my brooding silences. She took life as it came, where as I liked to plan, to be precise. Over the years we brought out the worst in each other, my affair just made that more apparent. But I decided to try one more time, and we moved to Los Angeles to give us a shot away from Serena. It hadn't worked and the long sunny days just highlighted the cracks in our relationship. I think Jen resented me moving her away from the life she'd built in San Francisco. Jen was spoiled, careless and she didn't care whose money she spent as long as she was having a good time. She had always been a bit materialistic but back then I didn't think much of it. Seeing who she ended up with was comical but I still wished her well.

Serena mentioning her only made me think of the differences between them and why I was so much more drawn to her than I ever was to Jen. It wasn't just physical, but the physicality highlighted their differences starkly. Where Jen was tall and very slim, Serena was petite, had curves that enticed me far more than Jen or Ceci. She had darker hair and captivating hazel eyes that haunted my dreams for years.

"Are you sure?" She questions me but I can see it's only a half ass attempt at distracting me.

I kiss her neck lightly again as my hand slowly travels down her body, to the edge of her skirt, "I'm sure. I only want you." It's the honest truth and she knows it.

She looks at me intensely as if she's trying to decide something and I know we're both playing with fire here but there's not much standing in the way of me having my way with her right now. She just had to say the words.

I can feel it; we're both so close to giving in, so close to just saying "fuck it". She tilts her head to the side as if inviting me to keep going and let this continue until we can't stop. Until we forget who we are, lost in the moment.

"You do things to me Serena…" I whisper as she leans into me more. Our bodies are pressed up against each other and my cock is hard against her stomach.

"Kaleb— God." She moans and I start to push her skirt up, my fingers trailing over her thighs.

Suddenly we hear voices outside and as fast as we can, we pull apart and straighten our clothes. Serena stares at me, a strange expression on her face and then there's a knock. I know she's wrestling with her inner demons about us, but she needs to see that what I'm offering her is worth the risk.

"Mr Collins, your meeting is starting soon." The receptionist calls from the other side of the door.

So I leave. In the boardroom there are a couple of familiar faces waiting for me. We talk about payroll and pretty much go over everything that we have already gone over before. It's draining really because I have to talk about it and listen to it all again. Serena is still in my office working, she didn't have to be at this meeting and I was kind of glad. It would've been hard to get through it with her next to me, tempting me with her presence.

I want to say screw it all and leave work right then and there and take Serena home with me already, but I hold back. At this point, I didn't think she'd protest— much. But I want her to be sure, to be desperate, to beg me.

So when the meeting ends I have Ceci bring in all the paperwork we have to prepare for the new hires and then I summon Serena.

Serena

Kaleb calls me into the boardroom and spread out in front of him I see piles of papers. I guess these are the induction forms and contracts I spent all day yesterday downloading and printing out for the new staff members starting tomorrow.

"We need to sort this out today." Kaleb said, his voice gravelly. Being in close proximity every day was beginning to take its toll, we were both horny, both frustrated and I was trying hard to resist him. In his office this morning we'd already had another close call. He was tempting me and I was trying to fight it but experience taught me that resisting Kaleb was futile. It was like trying not to breathe. This morning he ended our embrace, he had let me off the hook. He was going easy on me and we both knew it.

I give him a small smile and I know that this afternoon will be different as he smiles back at me, a mischievous gleam in his eye. I walk towards him, swaying my hips slightly and stop just to his left. He quickly explains what he wants in each welcome pack and hands me a stapler. As our fingers touch, our eyes lock and I can feel the spark that passes between us. Reaching for the first pack, I start arranging papers as Kaleb stands to the side of me sending emails on his phone.

His hand slides down my spine absentmindedly and rests on the curve of my ass. Part of me wants to call him on it, but the other part wants him to carry on. To strip me naked and worship me right here in the boardroom. To touch me like he loves me.

"Thinking naughty things Serena?" He asks leaning in close to me, his body pressed up against mine as he puts his phone down on the table. His hand is still on me practically burning my skin through my clothes.

"Maybe." I say. Two can play at this game. I am not a scared little mouse afraid that he's going to leave again. I am not the same person he left behind three years ago. I know that this will never be serious, not for him.

"Good." He squeezes my ass cheek, "So am I."

God I can feel myself blushing as my body stiffens. I want him inside me. Now. But we're professionals, and we're playing with fire so I ignore his comment and carry on arranging the paperwork into induction packets, one for each new employee. I bend across the desk, letting the curve of my behind brush against his groin. I may not be as forthcoming with words as he is, but that doesn't mean I can't have a little fun of my own, especially after what he did to me this morning in the office.

"Serena, you're killing me. The things I want to do to you on this table, in full sight of everyone…"

I straighten back up, almost leaning into him but not quite touching. Biting on my bottom lip, I realize that he's intoxicating, I'm addicted and right now he's driving me wild.

"Tell me then." I say coyly, turning to look at him. I see a fire in those cool blue eyes and I know I'm so wet now, I can feel my body wantonly responding to him. It's like he sees straight through me and into my core, setting a blaze there that I can't escape.

He grins and I feel my heart flutter. Even now that smile still makes my insides turn to mush. I face away, and he wraps his arm around my waist, closing the already small space between us.

His mouth is inches away from my neck as he whispers "I'd lift you on to the edge of the table, slowly move that pencil skirt up…"

His teeth catch the lobe of my ear and he gently

nibbles. I let out a soft moan, as his lips move from my ear to the curve of my neck. I picture him in his office this morning, his hands on my thighs as he pushed up my skirt.

With another nip he carries on, "You're wet for me, as I peel off your thong, slide them down those sexy legs and kneel before you…"

His hand trails up my body to cup my breast through my shirt and my whole body hums beneath his touch. I can picture everything he says, and I'm craving more. I imagine that he demands that I part my legs for him, before he hooks my left leg over his shoulder.

I know he's thinking the same as me because we've been here before; this isn't our first tango. His fingers begin to circle my nipple, still through my blouse and I'm itching to throw caution to the wind and unbutton my shirt, but I don't. I want to see where this is going.

"We can't do this." I say unconvincingly. My protests are growing weaker with every encounter we have, pretty soon there'll be no point in even trying.

"You don't say that in my fantasy," He replies as he pinches my swollen nub, "Instead you beg me for more as you feel the warmth of my breath on that perfect pussy of yours. I use my fingers to feel how wet you are, before tasting you. Serena, God…you taste amazing." He kisses my neck, before dragging his teeth over the sensitive skin there.

I exhale slowly, this man will be the death of me, I'm sure of it.

"As my tongue finds your clit I slide a finger inside you— you're so fucking tight, it's driving me crazy." I can feel his erection pressed into my ass and I grind against him. There's a knock on the door and we spring apart, the moment ruined.

Again.

KALEB

Damn it!

All this sexual tension is driving me up the fucking wall. Despite all of the interruptions, I'm surprised Serena hasn't caved. It isn't like it was before, I don't want to just meet up after work every day again, this time it would be more than just casual sex. She'd be mine forever, so I waited for her to say something, anything but it didn't come. A part of me wants her to say she doesn't love Sean, that there is only me but she isn't ready yet. My jealousy grows every time she's in my arms, every time we kiss. She is mine, and I am hers but she needed to stop fighting it.

Now with the Christmas party upon us I wasn't sure if I wanted to put myself through all of that teasing just to have her pull back once again. She'd been avoiding me the last three days, working with Mary or Sharon. I think about this as I pick up my suit from the dry cleaners and then my phone rings.

"It's Kaleb." I answer automatically thinking it may be work again but it's not.

"Honey!" The high-pitched voice on the other end makes me cringe for a minute.

I smile as I get into my car, "Mother. How are you?"

She makes a sound, "How do you think? You haven't visited me in a while and Christmas is coming up. Are you going to come home?"

Before answering, I have to think about it because the store is on the verge of opening and I have to be around to make sure things run as smoothly as possible and on top of that— there's Serena. I know she has family but I don't know what her plans are or if Sean is even part of them. Of course Sean is a part of them, he's her *fiancé*. I shake my head at my own wishful thinking.

"Mom, I'm not sure. I want to visit but I have to make sure work is good before I can make a decision. How's the family?" I know she's going to get whippy about it if I don't tell her I'll be there so changing the subject quickly was the only thing to do.

She sighs, "Same as usual. Your father is working right now but he wanted me to tell you that he needs to talk to you about the property in New York."

I roll my eyes at the mention of New York,

"Mom, I don't want that property. Tell Christian, he's older and can probably do more with it—"

"No, your brother is too busy for that. Anyway, when you visit we can talk about it."

"*If* I visit, I'll tell you in person what I just told you." I say dryly. My family has been in the real estate business for ages, my brother took after dad and he's always done what they wanted him to do. I, on the other hand had always done the opposite but it wasn't like I went out of my way to. I was just more interested in the more hands on side of a business than just designing and selling properties. Even though it had made our family successful, it was just boring to me. This property she was talking about just happened to be in the upper east side of New York and it was inherited but everyone in the family liked California more than New York, it's where our family was from. Somewhere back history the Collins family lived on the other side of the US and although it's what helped our family get where we are today, no one wanted to bother with it. It wasn't in the best shape either so someone had to go over there and see what could be done about it. Well, that someone wouldn't be me.

"We'll see." She laughs for a moment, "Are you bringing someone?"

"Mom I told you—"

She doesn't let it go, "If you come? Are you seeing anyone?" She's just curious, and it still bothers me that I can't tell her everything. I didn't think she'd want to know the truth. An affair wouldn't sit well with my uptight family.

"Don't think so." I say automatically. What were the chances that Serena would get to meet my family in the next couple of weeks? None.

"I was just wondering. It's been a long time since you were with *Jen*." She doesn't give anything away but I know she's glad that I'm not with her anymore.

My mother is a kind woman but just like everyone she had her bad side and Jen seemed to bring that out in her. Ever since they first met she'd disliked Jen and she had warned me that Jen was a 'fake person'. She told me discreetly that she didn't want to see much of her. That drove a wedge between us because by keeping Jen away, I also had to stay away. Since the break-up I've tried to visit more but now with my job being here I didn't have much of a choice in the matter.

"There *is* someone special but she won't be able to make it because of work." The words were out of my mouth before I thought about what I was saying. I loved my mom and I didn't mind her knowing that

Serena was someone special to me. Even if she couldn't be with me.

"Lovely! I hope I get to meet her soon though and that you can come for Christmas. Call me back when you find out if you can." She finally says.

I get off the phone then, go home to shower and change. With my mind made up, I decide that Serena has to want me more than ever. She should feel how I feel every time I'm near her. With her I want forever, but I can't keep pushing her. She's about to be the one that comes to look for me this time around.

It's going to happen.

Serena

I pull the dress over my curves, it's a little snug but that's what I'm after. Laura stops for a moment when she comes into the dressing room and wolf whistles as she steps forward to do up the zip.

"Damn, you look good Rena." she says grinning and I have to admit that I do.

In fact I look amazing. The red material dips near my cleavage, hugging my breasts and giving me a Jessica Rabbit appearance. The skirt clings to my waist and then flows out just past my hips, leaving chiffon fabric swishing around my ankles and when I move you notice a split that goes all the way up to my thigh, exposing my tanned skin.

I twirl in the mirror, I wouldn't usually go for something strapless and in this shade of red, but I didn't want to take it off. I needed this dress. I loved this dress. Sod the expensive label, I was worth it. I was definitely going to turn heads at the work Christmas party.

"Sean's going to love it." Laura assures with a hint of disdain in her voice. She had always hated Sean and the feeling was mutual. She would always point out if she thought he was putting me down or being unkind. But she knew how much he meant to me, so they put up with each other to a degree. I didn't push it and kept them as separate as I could, something that was easier these days with Sean working away every couple of weeks.

Before I could stop the words from leaving my mouth, they'd slip out and I whisper, "It's not for him."

Her eyes widen as she looks at me, and then she bursts out laughing. "Good!"

She didn't ask who it was for but I think she already knew. I met Laura at a yoga class I took to try and fill my spare time after Kaleb left and she knew that he was my new boss. She was a typical hopeless romantic and said I should have followed him, or refused to let him leave. In her eyes I should have done anything but stay with Sean. She said this was our second chance at love. But I made my choice back then and I have stood by that for the last three years, however things are different. Something is changing and I'm not sure what is in store for Sean and I. Our relationship feels empty, my life feels empty. It's not normal to feel this numb over everything and Kaleb, well Kaleb breathes a fire into me that consumes me from the inside. He makes me burn.

I shimmy out of the dress and give her a grin of my own as I throw my jeans and blouse back on. I was buying this dress, and some new shoes. Heck maybe I'd even wear that sexy lace bustier I bought last month for my weekend getaway with Sean. Not long after I checked-in to the little hotel, he rung to say he'd been called away for work. The bustier had sat in its box, carefully wrapped in tissue paper awaiting its debut since then. Why let such a gorgeous piece of underwear go to waste?

When we get to the checkout I pull out my savings card. The money I'd saved over the years, plus the money my parents gave me when I decided that college wasn't for me, meant that I'd had enough to cover the deposit on the house and still leave a little something in the bank for me to treat myself now and again. I'd been adding to it over the years, hoping to have a little nest egg for when we started a family. This was a treat I deserved, I worked hard and I'd had a promotion, so I feel no guilt as I slide my card into the reader.

Only the card is declined. I try it again. Declined.

I apologize to the cashier and pull out my other card and put it on there instead blushing profusely. I should have money on there, the card must be damaged I mutter to myself as the payment clears. They bag up my dress and shoes, handing it over with a smile but I feel embarrassed and confused. That shouldn't have happened.

After a few moments of silence as we walk to the car Laura asks me, "What's the matter?"

"My card, it shouldn't have been declined." I say angrily as I shove the bag in the backseat of her Volkswagen.

"Maybe you overspent?"

"I never use it. There should be a couple of grand on there Lau."

She frowns at me as we climb into the car. By the time she drops me off home I've rung my bank and made an appointment, because of the holidays they are behind and I can't get in to see them for two weeks. In the meantime they've frozen the account and they're going to send me my latest statements, but God knows when I'll get them, my bank is notoriously slow.

Something isn't right here, and I can feel it tugging at the back of my mind but I push it aside.

Tomorrow is the Christmas party and I am going to enjoy myself, this isn't going to taint my night.

KALEB

I've been trying to stay professional but it's hard to when Serena looks so damn good in everything she wears but I keep it in my pants, barely. So when she walks into that party in a red dress, looking like a goddamn queen, I freeze. I can't help but stare and I'm sure everyone else in the room is too but I don't pay any attention to them. Then our eyes meet and she's all that matters. The sizzle of electricity that practically crackles audibly between us tells me that tonight she feels the same way I do. There's something in her eyes; it almost looks like determination. No other man in the room has her attention.

It's hard but I turn away because I don't want to show her how much she affects me. Not when I've shown my hand already and she must know how I feel about her. None of that matters tonight. I'm done playing these silly games. There's no room for that because she's going to offer herself up to me on a silver fucking platter.

She'd been playing hard to get this whole time, pushing me away just enough but still letting my hands roam all over her body. It was driving me wild. I was beginning to think that maybe she didn't want me after all, but I'm going to find out just how far Serena is willing to go tonight. Not just with sex, the whole package.

We have a connection, we've always had it and no matter how much distance I tried to put between us she was always on my mind. We've been flirting and teasing each other since she started working with me and I wanted her to know, to *feel* how much she really means to me.

Someone taps my shoulder and I was hoping it's Serena, but it was just Ceci. I swear I can't get away from that woman.

"Kaleb, you look handsome as always." She winks, her hand placed on my arm as she leans in to whisper in my ear, "Maybe later we can catch up?"

I catch Serena's questioning eyes across the room but I glance back at Ceci and pull away, "I think we discussed everything about the project last time we had a chat. Unless I need to go over anything else with you, then *we're done*."

Not giving Ceci an opportunity to say anything more, I turn away and look for Serena but she wasn't where she was a few seconds ago. Great, I curse under my breath. Ceci was determined to ruin everything. Serena probably thought there was still something going on between us. There isn't and there never will be. I needed to have another a little chat with Ceci one of these days, she clearly wasn't taking the hint. I didn't want her and unfortunately for her, the next chat we'd have wouldn't be one she wanted.

I walk around the room talking here and there with other co-workers until eventually I'm bored. Serena has been watching me, I've caught her staring several times from the bar but I have made up my mind, I wouldn't go to her. This time she's going to come to me.

Grabbing a drink I walk outside to the patio. I may look confident as shit, like I usually do, but inside I'm praying that she comes. I don't know what the next step is if she doesn't. The thought that she might not actually want me is beginning to feel too real right now.

"Nice night out, isn't it?" Serena's soft voice comes from behind me.

I smile to myself and nod, letting out a small sigh of relief. Score one to Kaleb.

"Enjoying the party?" She tries again.

"Are you?" I ask in return, keeping my voice level and detached.

She walks around to stand by me and we're both looking out into the night. There's some lighting outside but it's still dark.

"I don't really know many people here, but it's nice." She replies.

I could hear it in her voice, there's something else she isn't saying. Is it nice to be away from Sean? I wonder if that's what she means but we don't need to talk about him so I don't ask. This is between us, there's no room for Sean here tonight.

"I'm glad you came." I tell her honestly, looking at her. I can't stay distant; I need to give her something so that she knows I'm not just playing with her.

Serena turns towards me and with the lighting from the party combined with the glow of the moonlight out on the dark patio, she looks like an exotic creature. I can't stop staring at her, the way the dress both floats around her and clings, the way her hair falls softly around her face— *all of it*. She's a vision.

Damn.

I wanted to peel that dress off her, leaving a trail of kisses across her body as the cool air washed over her exposed skin but unfortunately we are surrounded by people. Not just any people either, but people we had to see again on Monday.

"Kaleb, sometimes you overwhelm me. I feel like you're trying to get inside my head and mess with me." She says quietly as some guys from accounts walk behind us and go back inside.

I reached out for her and gave her a no-nonsense look to take my hand. She did. Without another word I pulled her around the building.

"Is this what you mean?" I ask as I push her gently against the wall and my hands trail lightly down her arm.

She has no place to go. If she felt overwhelmed before, well she was going to feel a whole lot more than that now.

Serena looks me in the eyes, "Kaleb, we can't keep doing this..."

I cock my head to the side, "We can't?" My hand slowly moves down her body.

She tries shaking her head but her breathing is heavy now, she's been on edge, I could tell. We both have.

"Mmm, I could take you right here, right now." I whisper in her ear as I press my body closer to hers, letting her feel all of me.

Serena

My breath catches as I feel his cock against my leg; the fabric of my dress pushed aside at the spilt so there's only one layer between us. I want him so bad. I grind against him just a little, letting him know that I'm barely holding on.

He catches the lobe of my ear between his teeth and I let out a soft groan, I need him inside me now, but we can't. Not here. Not now. I can hear music drifting out from the party, voices and laughter carrying on the breeze but out here we were in our own little bubble. I reach down and run my hand over his length, I can feel him twitching beneath my hands. It seems he's just as eager as me.

"Don't push me" He growls into my neck, pressing himself further into my body. We're up against the wall and it feels like we're melting into each other, lost in limbs and urgency as his lips crash down on mine claiming my mouth. His kiss is raw, it's like he's angry with me. Punishing me for the years we've been apart.

Kaleb reaches around and grabs my ass, squeezing and massaging as his kiss is unrelenting. I move into him, pressing my breasts against his chest, wanting to be closer although we physically can't get any nearer to each other unless we were naked. The thought excites me even more. His hand runs over the bare flesh on my leg, and I am so glad I bought this dress. The split in the skirt gives him easy access as his fingers move higher up my thigh, teasing me. As his fingers reach the edge of my panties, he pauses. He breaks away from our kiss, and looks at me intently and I can see the desire on his face, I love that not letting go is just as hard for him as it is for me. He's been chasing me since day one but now he was holding back and waiting for my surrender.

"Are you sure?" He asks seriously and I want to scream at him. I haven't felt like this in a long time.

"Yes!" I moan, kissing him,

He pulls away again, "Serena, there's no going back after this."

I take his hand and practically shove them inside my panties so he can feel how much I want this. His fingertips graze against my pussy and he lets out a moan of his own when he feels the wetness there. It was too late, I was lost to him the moment I saw him again.

I can feel him grinning in the darkness, the shadows hiding us from anyone who might come outside. He peppers a trail of kisses down my neck, on my collarbone as his index finger rubs against my opening, I need him now but he's determined to take his sweet time.

He nibbles on my lower lip, grazing his teeth against the soft flesh and I let out a noise of annoyance. He chuckles at me, *he fucking chuckles.* Snaking my hands through his hair I pull his head closer to mine and I can taste hints of the whiskey he's been drinking as my tongue meets his.

He finally gives in, sliding a finger inside me while his thumb grazes against my clit almost making my legs buckle. This man is all I ever wanted I think to myself as he begins to move slowly in and out of my body. As he moves faster, my hips begin to thrust of their own volition towards him, my body wanting more as I'm pinned against the wall. I want all of him inside me, but that isn't going to happen here.

KALEB

She came to me. That makes me happy and what's even better is I'm giving her what she's asking for. I know she wants more, I do too but right now this is what I'm going to do to her. Her legs tremble as she gets closer and closer.

"Do you want me Serena?" I pull my finger out for a minute because I want to know *now*, "Tell me." I order looking into her half shut eyes.

She whimpers, "Kaleb..."

I push my fingers in her mouth and she sucks the juices right off, greedily slurping against my hand and then I kiss her lightly on the lips. Fuck that was hot.

"Tell me." I whisper firmly in her ear.

This moment will tell me everything I *must* know. My finger circles her clit and she closes her eyes for a second.

"Yes." Her voice is small and I have to pause and look at her to check if I heard her right.

"Look at me and say it again," I tell her, my finger is lingering right around her opening now.

"Yes. I *want* you Kaleb." She says a little more loudly this time.

I push my finger inside her again, and this time I don't stop. She's holding in her cry and I kiss her as her orgasm comes. Our tongues dance with each other as she lets go and her body arches off the wall.

We're both breathing hard and I'm not thinking clearly. All I know is that she's mine forever now and as her orgasm passes, I hold her in place.

"I love you." I whisper in her ear. The words are out of my mouth now, I hadn't intended to say them— but it was too late. I can't take them back. I meant them, I do love her but Serena says nothing. She freezes in my arms and I just hold her. We stay like that for a minute or two but then I have to go, I can't process what I just said. It wasn't supposed to happen like that. What if I've scared her away?

I pull away from Serena and leave her leaning against the wall because I can't talk about it right now. I walk away. Again.

It was the only thing I could think to do because she said nothing. Her silence was deafening. To tell her how I feel so soon was a rookie mistake. Operation 'Happily Ever After' just took a hit. I shake my head as I drive home, there was no way I was going back to the party and I can't even look at Serena. If she didn't feel the same I wasn't sure what I was going to do. Did I want to keep pursuing her if she wanted to stay with Sean and I was just an occasional someone that could give her a good time? Could I do that?

I shake my head again because she wouldn't do that. I wouldn't do that. It would kill me. There was nothing I could do to change what happened; instead I just hoped that she would come around. I prayed that she felt the same way.

Serena

Kaleb disappears into the crowd and then he's gone. He tells me he loves me and then leaves, and I don't know what to say, how to feel. My head is spinning not only from the orgasm but his revelation. He never told me that he loved me before, not the last time. Now we're both changed, and I can feel it in the way he looks at me, the way he touches me. Before, our affair only brought sadness and hurt and we knew it had to end but now it's like there is a glimmer of hope for us, somehow— someway.

I call for a cab home because I'm not sure I trust myself to walk and I'd probably end up at Kaleb's apartment, demanding to know what he meant by confessing his love for me. I needed to wait or I could ruin everything. Just a little longer.

I know Sean will still be up, he always stays up late working these days but I'm not sure if he remembered about the Christmas party. When I'd mentioned it to him he'd been glued to his phone as per usual. Sean's job was slowly taking over our 'together time', his phone constantly buzzing and he'd just flash me a charming apologetic smile and say 'time zones' as if that magically explained everything.

The guilt creeps in as my house comes into view, what I've done tonight – what Kaleb said— it's changed things. I need to start figuring out what I'm going to do and how I'm going to leave. I put my key in the door and take a deep breath, I never know which Sean I'm going to get when I come home.

He's lying on the couch watching TV when I get in; it's just gone eleven. I'm taking off my heels by the door and tying up my hair in the hallway mirror as he calls out "You look... happy."

I give him a small smile but say nothing. He's drunk. I can see several cans on the carpet and even though I can't see it, I can smell a greasy pizza. So much for his clean eating habit. Any traces of guilt I felt about what happened this evening have vanished, evaporating like the alcohol fumes coming off my supposed future husband.

"Where have you been?" He asks, grabbing my wrist as I walk past the sofa to the stairs. His eyes sweep my body but not in the same way that Kaleb looked at me, no this was like disapproval.

"I told you, the work Christmas party. It was… interesting. I had a great time." I'm trying to stay calm and pull away but I can see Sean is trying to start something with me. He's just itching for a fight but I'm not ready for him to ruin my night.

"Yeah, bet it was." He lets go of me, practically shoving my arm back at me.

"What does that mean?" I eye him warily, I'm stepping into the trap he's laying for me and we both know it.

"Nothing." He turns away and back to the TV screen, the flashing images lighting up the dimly lit living room. I can't stand it when he's like this. He flips between confrontational and passive aggressive, then he'll finish it with the silent treatment, intending to make me feel awful until I cave and apologize.

"How much have you had to drink? You smell like a brewery." I try to deflect away from me, and my night. I don't want Sean to know about Kaleb and me yet.

"I may have had a few." He grins and it's sinister, twisted. It's not like the calm, loving Sean that I used to know and my heart almost stops for a moment.

"I think it's time for bed Sean." I say, trying to be stern but calm.

"I don't think it is *Serena*." He says mimicking my

tone before falling silent. He sits on the sofa and stares at me, his dark eyes burning into me. I decided the best thing to do is ignore him, so I leave, not saying a word and go upstairs. Moments later and the door slams – Sean is gone again.

KALEB

If someone had told me that I'd be back in Serena's life after leaving her that night at the hotel room three years ago, I would've laughed. I never would have believed it. But as the days dragged on I realize that I never should have left. Now, I wasn't just back in her life but we were working together and I'm closer to making her mine. Just mine.

I've always loved Serena. Even back when I was with Jen, I felt guilty but I couldn't stop caring about her. She was *The One*. I didn't stay away from Serena when I was supposed to; the Facebook stalking wasn't the worst of it. One day I even saw her. It was from a distance and only because I had to pick up a suit I'd ordered online at a store in the same shopping center she happened to be in. It was when we had started talks and holding meetings about opening a store here.

That was the day I'd bought the ring. The ring I had caught Serena staring at in a jewelry store. She'd even tried it on, looking at it longingly but quickly handed it back once she saw the price. After she'd left, I couldn't help myself. I went in there and asked to see the same ring up close. It was definitely her taste, simple but beautiful. In the end it wasn't a hard decision to make. I'd made a down payment on it and paid it in full before I left town again.

Even then, I didn't really believe I'd ever get her back. Now that I was here and everything seemed to be going the way I wanted it…needed it to go, I wasn't about to back down. I told her I loved her and it was true. Okay, so I didn't plan to tell her so soon but if she felt anything for me it wouldn't make a difference to the end game.

The only problem was that dickhead, Sean. He was a ticking time bomb and I wasn't sure how much longer I'd be able to keep everything a secret. In the back of mind my guilty conscience almost ruined every moment I was with Serena because all I could think about were the consequences of lying to her. The whole damn reason I'd left in the first place was because of Sean. She was going to find out sooner or later, I knew it was a matter of time. And now I didn't know if she'd ever see that ring. Would she marry a liar? Would she see that I'd tried to protect her this entire time or would it all backfire on me?

Serena

Sean's behavior recently has me on edge; I have no patience for his drinking or his temper tantrums. I can't stand the guilt trips and the cold looks he gives me every time he glances my way. He's the one pushing *me* away and I guess I'm glad; it makes what I have with Kaleb easier. Kaleb makes me smile. He makes me feel flustered and excited all at once. After the Christmas party it's clear where this is headed, and to be honest it's a little overdue. I can't remember when I had sex last, when I felt wanted and every inch of me felt alive. But Kaleb does that to me, he turns my brain to mush until Sean is nothing but a regretful afterthought. I know I'm a horrible person— I just want one thing that's mine, I want for one moment to feel like the old me. With Sean I feel so empty and I know that it's not right; I know we should end it but it's not that simple, it never is. What happens when it does? Kaleb never wanted my love before, but this time it feels different. It's changed and so have we, but what does that mean for us?

"You're different." I say looking at Kaleb, giving my thoughts a voice "You've changed since you left." He's standing behind his desk, with another sharp suit on, looking every inch the assertive businessman. Since the Christmas party and the incident with Ceci, I realized that Kaleb had changed a lot more than I originally thought. And it was good, he was confident and it made him sexier, irresistible, as if I wasn't struggling with that as it is. Working with him was becoming harder, especially since he told me he loved me which neither of us was acknowledging but I couldn't stop thinking about him, his mouth on my body, his fingers inside me. I was desperate for more, it was like he'd woken up a sleeping, horny dragon and I didn't know how to control the appetite that was growing each time he touched me. And he was taking every opportunity to touch me, to glance over my body like a hungry wolf and at times I could swear he was baiting me.

"Different how?" He asks, placing some paperwork down.

I tilt my head slightly as I look him up and down, "You're more blunt, bossy."

"Bossy?" He arches a brow at me, taking a step closer.

"Commanding." I reply simply.

"Does that scare you?"

"No…" I say slowly before deciding to be honest, "Yes."

"Does it excite you?" He's standing behind me now, his breath warm on the back of my neck.

I flick my tongue out to lick my lips; I can feel his breathing hitch as I do so.

"Yes." I whisper.

"Does that make you wet for me?"

I say nothing. He is definitely baiting me. It's working though because I am wet for him all over again and my body aches to be touched. But he keeps his hands to himself; the warm trickle of air as he exhales is the only thing I can feel.

"Turn around." He demands.

And I do, leaning back on the edge of his desk.

He kneels before me, slipping each foot gently out of my heels one at a time. How could removing my shoes be so damn erotic? I was almost begging for him to touch me. Seconds later I get my wish as Kaleb's hands work their way up my thighs, gently massaging my skin as they move higher and higher. This man will be the death of me and I know I've said it before but it's true, I muse as I watch them disappear beneath my skirt. I'm surprised my clothes are still on to be honest, Kaleb always used to like to get as close to me as he could— clothes were usually the first thing to go. A lot has obviously changed in the last three years.

His knuckles brush against me through the thin fabric of my thong and I quickly decide that I like this new, tempting, more refined Kaleb. All his teasing over the last few weeks has made me desperate for him. I arch my back into him, wanting him to touch me again but the bastard just grins and slips my panties down my legs before tossing them to the floor. I wait with baited breath for him to return to touching me but instead his hands slide up to my waist holding me in place as he claims my mouth with his.

I'm growing impatient as I unbutton his trousers and push them down past his hips and to the floor. I meet his gaze as I realize he's gone commando, his cock hard and I take that as proof that he wants me like I need him. I can feel my body itching for more. I push Kaleb back into his office chair and smile wickedly at him. He knows what I want; he's always been able to read me like a book— that much hasn't changed.

I straddle him, feeling his dick against me, seeking a way in. Neither one of us speaks but we communicate by touch alone. I lick my lips at this and position myself so that I can lower my body down on his cock. The feeling is intense, everything burns and my skin feels like it's been set alight, every nerve begging for release. Once I have the full length of him inside me I let out a little groan, this man is delicious. I feel complete for the first time in years, I feel like I can finally breathe. I begin to rock my hips slowly, moving myself up and down on his length while he just watches, not saying a word. This is feral, a raw passion and he knows how badly I want this. I can tell that he's afraid if he breaks the silence I'll stop, but I can't stop. I don't want to.

Tonight I'm after my own orgasm and he's just along for the ride. This is the first time we've been together in years, it's frantic and frenzied, there's no time for nice and romantic. It isn't like the Christmas party either where he was in charge.

It's been so long since I've felt like this that I almost come too quickly. Taking a deep breath I slow the rolling motion of my hips, trying to regain control. Kaleb thinks I'm trying to pull away to stop so he reaches up and pinches my nipples through my blouse. He quickly pops open a few buttons and frees my breasts from the lacy confines of my bra. I'm still partially dressed, my skirt has been pushed up around my waist and right now that's adding to the atmosphere. I feel filthy, sexy, wanted. I bite on my bottom lip as he cups each breast, squeezing them before pinching my nipples again, drawing out a wild moan from my mouth. The point where our bodies meet is slick with juices; this is what Kaleb does to me. He fucks with my mind almost as well as he fucks my body.

KALEB

This was beyond my vision of fucking her on my desk over and over again. She took control; she straddles me like her life depends on it. This woman was everything I could dream of and then some. Every other woman in my life had been bland compared to her.

I knew she wasn't as experienced, having been with only two men in her life, but by God did she know exactly what to do and how to do it. Serena was made for sex, her body luscious and curved. The way she tucked a stray piece of hair behind her ear, the way she licked her lips – fuck, the way she walked even made me hard. It was intoxicating the way she oozed sinfulness. She bounced on my cock like she was trying to pump me dry; she was consuming me, devouring me all with the thrust of her hips. Was it like that with Sean? I push that thought away quickly for a later time.

Serena pulls me forward and I know exactly what she wants.

"More." She rasps, her breathing uneven.

My mouth closes around her right nipple and I tease her with my tongue before I move on to her left. I can tell she's desperate for me, like a sex starved addict and I'm surprised she's riding me so hard, but she takes it all, every inch of me as I lift my hips slightly to match her rhythm.

A soft mewling noise lets me know Serena was about to come and honestly I'd been waiting for her to, I didn't know how much longer I was going to last. She was so fucking sexy and beautiful, I wanted to tell her but I was afraid that it'd ruin the moment. Instead I take her face in my hands kissing her hard.

"Kaleb..." She says against my lips as her hands fist in my shirt and I know she's going over the edge.

Her head tilts back as she moans loudly and I'm glad everyone has left for the day or they would've heard us. The chair moves around with our out of control fucking as she comes hard.

As her orgasm rocks her she grips me tighter and I grin. The tightness from her pussy clamping down on me as she rides out the ripples of her climax sends me over the edge as I come, filling her up. In this moment we were one, a tangle of limbs all spent and sweaty from the mind-blowing sex. It was the kind of sex that got under your skin and left you feeling raw and broken. It was what fed our addiction to one another in the beginning, this time though there was love. Serena needs me just as much as I need her; she just wasn't prepared to admit it. Resting her head against my shoulder she relaxes into me, still partly undressed. I want this, this moment and I want it always. I don't say anything, I'm afraid of telling her that I love her again and not getting the same in return. I don't think I could handle that right now, not after this.

A vibrating noise interrupts our post-sex bliss and I don't even have to look at the caller ID to know that it's Sean. She stiffens against me, climbs off my lap and scoops up her thong. Dressing hastily she doesn't look at me. Every time I give her space she doubts my intentions, she doubts us. She's running home to him like the good little wife-to-be that she is trying to be. And I let her.

Serena

I'm trying not to think about Kaleb, about what we did yesterday in his office. My body may look the same but it didn't feel the same. I felt invigorated, like I'd been for one of those brutal massages where they pull you apart and then put you back together again. I felt like a new person...no, not new, just like the old me, the me before I became worn down and tired. Kaleb didn't try to make me do anything his way yesterday, he gave me the space to take what I needed. He didn't try to come first or to rush me like Sean does, not that we even have sex anymore.

All I can think about is Kaleb, I have to focus. I can't stop myself though and I'm picturing his hands on me, his mouth on mine even as I'm driving to the bank to sort out my card issues. I remember the taste of his kisses, sweet like cinnamon with the hint of coffee as always. He drinks too much coffee. I think about how his mouth claimed my nipple, sucking and biting. It's like he's wormed his way in and now I'll never be free. Kaleb is my drug of choice and while I abstained for three years, I was never really cured of my addiction. My mind is filled with only him as I park on autopilot, as I walk in and wait for my appointment. Is he thinking of me? What does this mean for us now? I know that I need to talk to Sean— but I'm not ready yet.

A soft cough brings me back to the present with a bump and I stare at the skinny man in the cheap black suit sat opposite me. My brain couldn't quite comprehend the slow drawn out things he was saying. God I hated bankers.

"So my money is still there?" I ask, hoping to get a clear answer from him.

He nodded, "Most of it yes."

"So why wouldn't my card work?" I frown, what did he mean most of it?

He makes a dismissive gesture with his hand and I can feel my blood beginning to boil.

"Because the money wasn't in there when you tried to use it." He gives me a patronizing look.

"I don't understand, you just said the money was there?"

"It's one of the reasons we froze your account Miss Davies. Random amounts of money were being withdrawn and then re-deposited back into the account days later. We view that as suspicious activity" He said gravely.

I nod, it was suspicious and I knew for a fact the only other person with access to my account was Sean. He must have a reason if he had been taking money from my personal account. My heart begins racing, did he know about Kaleb and I? Was he punishing me? Was this it? If he was preparing to leave me then I would finally be free to be with Kaleb. I'd already made that decision, but finding the right time to tell Sean was virtually impossible when he was never home these days. Work was keeping him away from me and in all honesty, I was grateful. It gave me the space to work out that our relationship wasn't going anywhere and it hadn't in a long time.

The banker handed me a folder of statements and told me that I could either give them to the police fraud team or I could look over it myself. I can't even remember the last time I looked at a statement for this account. I thank him even though he was less than helpful, telling me my money would be untouchable until the issue was resolved, and I leave.

Today has been one of those days that I could have done without. Kaleb had been fine about me taking a personal day, but Ceci had given me daggers all afternoon yesterday and quite frankly she was starting to piss me off. She must have known there was something more between us because her chilly attitude towards me had ramped up several notches since the party.

I needed some caffeine in my system STAT so I head for the nearest coffee shop. As I wait for my Mocha Frappuccino to be brought over I glance at the folder. Did I want to know? If it really was Sean did I need the hassle? But curiosity got the better of me and I pulled out the bundle of papers, stapled neatly into months. Looking over the figures I was confused, it was like the man at the bank had said large chunks of money and I mean a couple of thousand at a time were being withdrawn at a place called 'The Den'. Days later it was being put back in. As I went further back into the year I realized that it wasn't always being put back or not the entire amount. The numbers were all over the place and I had a sneaking suspicion why.

KALEB

"Kaleb?" Ceci's annoying nasally voice distracts me from finishing up work for the day. I take my eyes off the computer screen and look up to see that she's let her herself in.

"Yes?" I say in an unpleasant voice. I've been working twice as hard to make sure our project is done on time. Serena not being able to come into work today was both a blessing and a curse. Even though she's been a distraction, a hot, sexy one and typically we worked well together, recently my head was in the gutter instead of on our deadlines. Today she had some things to take care of and I know by the look on her face that it must have been important so I focus on our job and don't realize what time it is until Ceci walks into the office.

"I didn't know you were alone. Want some company?" She smiles or tries to smile seductively but I just roll my eyes. I'm tired of her lame attempts to get my attention.

"Ceci, please stop." I stand up as she freezes in front of my desk.

She seems shocked at first but recovers quickly, "What do you mean? Am I not your flavor tonight?" She places a hand on her hip as she waits for my response.

I frown, "What are you talking about now?"

She sighs, "Oh please, you and that new girl. Did you screw her on the desk too? Fuck her right here in this very office where you and I—" She stops mid-sentence as the door to the office opens.

Serena stands there staring at me with disappointment written all over her face.

"I'm sorry for interrupting." She mumbles as she turns to leave. I could see the tears in her eyes. I wanted to follow her, my heart aching just thinking about the pain I was causing her but I couldn't, not until I dealt with Ceci.

"Oh so it's more than just screwing—"

"You don't know what you're talking about," I move around my desk and look at her seriously, "This is the last time I'm telling you— leave me alone. Whatever happened before meant nothing and if you so much as look at Serena the wrong way, I'll make sure HR has a little talk with you about harassment. And Ceci…I won't stop there." I hadn't meant to threaten her but she was testing me. Enough is enough. I know it's my own damn fault, sleeping with her had been a mistake but she was threatening my chance with Serena. She was messing with the game when she didn't even know what was at stake.

Ceci shrinks back and steps away from me. "I understand." She whispers as she gives me one last longing look and leaves my office.

I'm on edge now. Damn Ceci for ruining the night and Serena...Shit. She probably still thought there was something going on between Ceci and I. There isn't, there is only Serena. She's everything and I was getting so damn close to making sure she knew that. I'll have to calm down before I try to explain to her that it's not what she thinks.

Why did she even come to the office? Did she forget something or was she there to see me? Isn't Sean at home waiting? I want to know.

I need to know.

Serena

I can't face Kaleb right now, and I can't think about him with Ceci. I send Laura a quick text and pick up some Chinese food on my way home. I need a friend; my life was becoming complicated. A part of me knew that Sean and I were over but I still had to actually make that final move. I was procrastinating, holding back for some reason. Seeing Ceci with Kaleb and over hearing them hurt, maybe he wasn't in this for the long haul and that scared me. He said he loved me, but did he mean it? I would be giving up everything, Sean, most probably my family and I'd have to transfer jobs too just to be with him and there he was in his office with her.

Laura's at my house before I am and I'm glad Sean's away with work on some training thing this week. He left last night so he could relax in the hotel and do a little sightseeing, at least that's what the note he left me said. We've both been working more than usual lately. Laura doesn't like coming around when he's here, and I swear sometimes he tries deliberately to make her uncomfortable. She grabs the takeaway bag from me as I let us into the house. She's soon dished up and is rummaging around my kitchen, pulling out a bottle of red wine and two large glasses. It isn't long before I've explained everything to her, the bank statements, the money moving, overhearing Ceci and Kaleb and how I was planning on breaking up with Sean. She knows better than to ask me about Kaleb, just saying his name was making me angry right now. I thought things were different this time around. How could I be so wrong? Instead we talk about my savings and what to do next as we sit on my sofa.

"You know what The Den is don't you?" Laura looked at me frowning before taking a sip of her wine.

I finish up the last of my beef chow mein and think about it for a moment before answering, "No but I think it's probably something to do with gambling."

She nods and part of me is glad because I know what I want to do next, but the other part is terrified. Does Sean have a gambling addiction? Does that mean he needs me more now than ever? The guilt stings because I know that I'm planning to leave, what if it destroys him?

"Yeah, it's downtown near that little boutique you like. The one with the ugly jewelry."

"Hey!" I love that shop, but Laura and I have very different styles. She's very relaxed and chic, whereas I agonize for hours over what to wear and how I look.

"Well it is. Who the heck wears felt necklaces? My three year old could make better." She snorts.

I raise an eyebrow at her and give a smile so that she knows I'm joking, "I've seen Daisy's paintings Lau, I hate to say it but your daughter isn't exactly Picasso."

She sticks her tongue out at me and I laugh. Tonight, wine and crap food is exactly the therapy I needed.

"So what do you want to do about this den place then?" She asks after a minute or two. I can see her out of the corner of my eye watching me, trying to gauge my emotions but I'm a mess. My head is all over the place and I feel like I'm being pulled in a million different directions.

I take a deep breath and slowly say, "I think I want to go there. Ask around. Find out what's really going on."

She just stares at me for a moment, her eyes wide

before she squeals, "Oooohh we're going to be investigators, like Watson and Holmes."

"Who?"

"Sherlock Holmes!" She exclaims squinting at me suspiciously, "I thought you were British!"

I laugh "By birth but I've lived here for years!"

"But Sherlock Holmes is famous!"

I just shrug and pour myself another glass of wine. Today has been a long ass day and I have a feeling things were only going to get worse.

KALEB

Serena hasn't answered any of my calls so I just leave her a voicemail and pray that she listens. She's probably still upset with me or maybe she's already in bed. I'm tempted to go to her house and find out what's going on but I quickly dismiss the idea. The last thing I want to do is cause a scene, stay calm Kaleb I tell myself over and over again. She just needs time. Instead I shut down my computer and leave the office, too distracted to do any more work.

Ceci left too. I was glad she didn't stick around because I didn't want to deal with her anymore. She knows I'm dead serious about the warning I've given her. Now I have to salvage my relationship with Serena. As I think over what I want to tell her in the morning, I stop dead in the middle of the parking lot. My eyes widen at the sight before me.

My car. It's been vandalized.

The windows were all there but the body of the

car – all ruined. Angry gashes and scratches cover every inch; it's as if something has clawed at it until there was practically no color left.

Jaw set and hands rolled into fists, I'm beyond furious. Who the fuck has the balls to do that? My mind races as I think about who could have done it. I know that for a fact this wasn't some kind of game or prank, it was personal. As I examine my car from all angles, I can think of only two people who could be responsible. Ceci or Sean. They're the only two on my shit list and I'm pretty sure I'm on theirs too. Both have reasons to hate me and both are malicious enough to do something like this.

It's a coincidence that Ceci left and now my car is damaged. If she saw it, why wouldn't she have come back in and said something? What about Serena? She would've seen it! Wait…no. She usually parks on the other side of the building, just another way to keep her distance from me at work. So that takes my thoughts back to Ceci, she usually parks near me, and her car is gone. All the cars were gone. Mine sits alone in the center of the parking lot. It's Ceci. It has to be.

But then what about Sean? He's supposed to be out of town this weekend, but who knows since he's always lying about his whereabouts. I know he suspects Serena and I are together again. So if he knows, he has reason to do it too.

"Damn it!" I shout to no one.

Someone is going to be very sorry they crossed me. I make a quick call to a mechanic I know who lives locally; those acquaintances I've racked up do come in handy at times. Plus, the mechanic looked over the engine and everything else for me. So when he tells me that the engine was faulty and it seems like it was intentionally done, I decide not to risk driving it. I get my car towed and call a cab.

Whoever has damaged my car really wants to hurt me and that bothers me because it means they're serious. And if this person is serious then they aren't going to stop here. What also concerns me is this was done at my place of work, outside but still, it's personal. I really don't want Serena to be around shit like that.

The only way to protect her is to find out who did it. I can't tell her, because if there's a chance it was Sean, for one I'd probably kill him and two, she'll need to know about everything but I can't stop the way her eyes light up when she looks at me, and I know that's selfish. I'm not ready for her to hate me.

Then there's Ceci. If it was her, she would've done

it out of jealousy and probably hated for how I talked to her. But would she really hurt me, or Serena? I couldn't be sure. I was going to have to keep quiet until I found out.

Serena

I'd left my phone upstairs all night, I didn't want to deal with Kaleb and Ceci but I also didn't want to talk to Sean either. Laura slept over so we stayed up late talking about anything and everything. She's been having relationship dramas of her own, but that was normal for her. No one was good enough for Laura, and if they were, they hated her daughter or vice versa. I loved Daisy but she could be a tiny terror when she wanted to be. That was the start of the night, a few bottles of wine later and we just ended up playing cheesy songs from when we were teens and singing along badly. Laura knew how to distract me, she knew that there was too much going on and if I talked about either of them, it would be like opening the floodgates.

I finally crawled up to my own bed at around 3am after making sure Laura was comfy in the spare room and by that I mean I took her shoes off for her and covered up her drunken ass with a duvet. As I pulled the covers around me, cocooning myself inside I finally listened to Kaleb's voicemail.

"It's not what you think. There's nothing between Ceci and I...Serena, you must know that. You...there's only you. Please let me know that you're not mad. Okay...I'll see you at work."

I curl my toes and have to muffle a little groan, it could be the wine or it could the way he says my name but this man gives me butterflies. When he said *'there's only you'* I could have melted, I mean, I knew that I was serious this time around. This just showed that he was too. It meant we had a real chance together; but that meant I had to end things with Sean. That thought scares me, I can feel a panic rising but I quickly push it down. I scroll through my texts and see that Sean's text me, each one getting more and more jumbled as the night went on. Obviously I wasn't the only one drinking tonight, the final text simply read 'Fck Youi'. I delete them and quickly text Kaleb to let him know I'm not mad. There's no response but then I'm not surprised, it is really late or really early depending on how you look at it.

I just hope everything works out; I need to get to the bottom of what's happening with my money. I need to talk to Sean. I resist the urge to call him, the wine and tiredness making me drowsy as I start to drift. I don't want to fight and I also don't want to tell him what I'm planning to do. I need evidence and tonight we made a plan of action on how were going to get it. I just hope Laura remembers it in the morning.

KALEB

I hardly sleep so I decide to just get up and get a workout in before I have to go and sort out a rental car. I still have to call my insurance and put in a claim on my wrecked car and I'm in a shitty mood. The only thing I didn't do is file a police report, I can't, at least not until I know who's responsible.

I put my earbuds in before cranking up the music, I'm going to try and run out my frustrations on the treadmill. Who the fuck would destroy my car like that? It wasn't just a scratch, done angrily with a key— it was ruined. What the hell did they use? My feet pound with every step and I increase the incline, it's not working and instead I'm getting angrier.

What really got to me the most is not being able to talk to Serena about it, especially after her text. It's all so fucked up and that pisses me off further because it seems like everything is hanging in the balance and I'm just here waiting for it all to come crashing down.

At any moment Serena could find out everything, and that's the thought lingering in the back of my mind.

I move on to do some weight lifting, but nothing seems to be taking the edge off. After some half assed reps I call it quits and head for the showers. I check my watch; Serena should be getting up about now. Is she at home showering too? Is Sean back yet? Did that dickhead trash my car? My blood boils now, and the cool water does little to calm me down.

Still, I push through and think about maybe spending more time with her outside of work. I know it's a risk but I want her for more than just her body. I need to show her that. I can give her so much more than he ever could. I fantasize about waking up next to her every day, about us living together finally. Those thoughts take a turn when I picture her underneath me, as I show her exactly what she does to me.

My cock hardens almost instantly and I stroke it as I think about her riding me again. Her moans, her tits bouncing, her shudders as she came. "Fuck." I say out loud and start pumping faster and faster. Imagining her sucking me dry as I close my eyes and I don't bother holding back, this is exactly what I need so I let go. Feeling a little less stressed and more in control of my emotions, I dress and head for the office, trying to think of ways I can convince Serena that I'm the one for her.

I plan while we work, in silence mostly. She's been lost in her own thoughts today and I don't want to pry so I leave her to it. It's a busy day and I know that I won't be able to taunt her today, to tease her until she's begging for me…we work straight through lunch. It doesn't matter though; we work so well together that just her company alone brightens my day. I guess that's also because we still flirt with each other. I'm more forward, cheekier in my comments because I enjoy seeing a blush creep up her cheeks as she struggles to act like it's not affecting her as much as it does.

And just like that I have the perfect plan.

Serena

Kaleb's watching me again and I can't think clearly. I'm trying to finish up these order forms by three pm or we'll have no stock in ready for the opening but his blue stormy eyes are fixating on me every few minutes; I can feel it when they land on me. It's like a burning sensation, as if he can see what's under my clothes and I know this isn't going to work. I can't concentrate when he's flirting with me and trying to get under my skin.

My phone rings and I'm grateful for the interruption. I mouth 'Sorry, need to take this' as I leave the room. His eyes darken as he assumes that it's Sean calling me. He's right – it is Sean and I sigh before answering.

"Hi. Is everything okay?" I frown. He should be almost home by now.

"Yeah. I just called to let you know that I need to stay here a few days longer." He sounds bored, like I'm an afterthought.

I can't stop the surprise in my voice as I say "Oh, okay. I thought you'd be home by now?"

"Something's come up, work wants me to stay." His tone is annoyed now. I hear a voice call his name in the background and some giggling. *Is he with a woman?* I shake my head pushing away the thought that he could be lying. It must be someone he works with.

"So when will you be back?" I ask.

"I don't know." He says slowly, talking to me as if I'm stupid.

"Rough guess?"

"Don't act like you give a shit Serena." And just like that he hangs up.

I stand in the corridor my mouth hanging open. I don't know what I've done to him to cause this. There's no way he can know about Kaleb and I. Besides he'd been acting strange even before I got the job. Maybe Laura was right, maybe Sean was trying to control me and now that his control was slipping he didn't like it. But…the Sean I met in when he was in college would never have done that. He was sweet, loving and he wanted my happiness above everything else. Had he really changed that much? There had to be something else causing his attitude.

I take a few moments to get myself together

before going back into the office. I feel rejected, humiliated and I know I have no right to. I'm also shocked by how tired and angry I feel. It's like Sean is sapping all the energy from me, leaving me broken. I know this has to end. I know that I need to claim myself back but I feel stuck. The intensity with which Kaleb offers me…I don't really know what he's offering me. He said he loved me but there's been no mention of a relationship or anything serious. But the way he makes me burn reminds me that there is more out there. I can't waste away in an average life as someone's average wife – I want to be someone's supernova.

When I walk back into the room and close the door behind me I know that Kaleb's face is going to light up like I'm the most beautiful thing he's seen in his whole life. I know that when he flirts with me, he sees only me. I know that with him, I can finally be me and that is worth burning out for.

KALEB

Up to this point there's been some pretty fucking hot moments, kisses in cupboards, we'd had sex in the office and I'd made her come up against a wall but there was something missing... Serena in my bed. I wanted to make love to her. I wanted to own every inch of her body, have her calling out my name while she was twisted in my sheets.

Now that I have her where I want her I know she won't say no to me. She can't. It's perfect timing really because when Serena comes back into the office she's shaking, she mutters something about how Sean had extended his "business trip" and then she carries on with her workload. I know the real reason behind his prolonged trip but I'm not about to tell Serena that.

I want us to spend the weekend together, starting with dinner tonight. I'd wine and dine her, romance her and then when Sunday came around she wouldn't want to go home. That was what I had been thinking about all day.

"What do you say you come over tonight and maybe spend the weekend with me?" Serena looks up from some paperwork she's focusing on.

"At your place?" She asks, curious. I'd never invited her before but this time around I wanted things to be different.

I was always worried about Sean finding out where I lived. Last thing I wanted was for that bastard to show up at my home, find Serena there and cause a scene. But since he was out of town, well let's just say I'd changed my mind.

"Yes." I reply simply.

She tilts her head for a moment and then smiles, "Okay."

"Great, I'll text you my address in a minute. See you at seven." I give her a lingering kiss on the lips before leaving her to get on with her work.

I have preparations to make for the night so I have to leave work early. I head to the liquor store and buy some wine and then I make my way to the supermarket and grab a few things for our dinner. Tonight I intended to wow her. By the time I get home and shower it's six o'clock, and Serena would be here soon.

I pull out some candles quickly and light them all around the house. It makes my flat look like an enchanted hideaway, the glow giving the place a magical feel.

Then I go back to the kitchen and set the table using a red tablecloth with gold settings, everything looks perfect. It's romantic and I'm pleased to see that I haven't lost my touch. By the time I'm done, it's already seven so I make a start on the food.

The doorbell rings a few minutes later as I'm chopping the garlic ready to add to the oil. I take the bottle of white wine out of the fridge, pull out the cork and let it breathe before I open the door.

Serena looks stunning in a simple, lacy, black dress that hugs her body in all the right places. Her dark hair is loosely pinned up, a few tendrils hang down framing her face and I want nothing more than to kiss her.

"Come in." I welcome her and move aside. Her perfume invades my house as she enters and I breathe in her scent, sweet hints of vanilla following her as she moves. She shrugs off her jacket and hangs it up before putting a small weekend bag down near the door.

"This is cozy." She says as she wanders around my home.

"It's the candles," I say grinning, "This way." I take her hand in mine and guide her into the galley kitchen.

"Have a seat while I make us dinner," I say with a low voice close to her ear.

"Mmm." She moans, nodding and that does things to me.

I resist the urge to kiss her and instead I pour her a glass of wine and switch on the music system. A soft jazz melody quietly fills the kitchen as I go around the island and continue to cook knowing she's watching me the entire time. Surprisingly she has a calming effect on me tonight, when we're away from the office and the pressure of Sean. At times it's like he's always with us, but not tonight. Tonight it's just the two of us.

"What are you making?" Her voice startles me for a second. I didn't hear her move but she stands close now, observing.

I glance back at her, "I'm making Yakisoba with chicken."

"What's that?" She looks at the pan as I stir all the veggies and noodles together,

"It's a Japanese stir-fry type of dish. It's one of my favorites." I wink at her as she sits on one of the stools. Serena smiles as she sips on her wine and I finish making our dinner.

"Do you own this place?" Serena's question catches me by surprise.

I dish up our plates and set them on the dining table, "No, it's a rental, although I have the option to purchase. At the moment, I don't see myself making that commitment."

Serena stares at me with a blank look on her face as she follows me to the table.

"What is it?" Did I say something wrong?

She sits down and avoids my gaze, "Wow. This looks so good!"

"Thank you." I sit and pour us both another glass of white but I'm still waiting for an answer, "Serena?"

She looks me in the eye, "It's just— I don't know how you did it. How you got out of the relationship you had with Jen. It seems so easy for you. Even now, you're free from commitments, from anything tying you here."

I'm confused by her words, is she telling me she wants to leave Sean? My heart beats faster at the thought. Is she telling me that she wants to be free and that she's choosing me? Or is she worried that I'll leave her like I did before because I've made no commitment to stay here? She *is* my commitment, my reason to stay.

"Serena, everyone has a choice. No one is tied anywhere, or to anyone— not really. Let's just enjoy tonight, it's the first time you've been to my home. Try the food." Just like that we move away from a dangerous subject. What I can't bring myself to tell her is that I wasn't purchasing a home without her. She was the only one I could see by my side. On some level she must have sensed that this time around I wanted her completely and wasn't going to give her up. At the same time, it was her decision to make.

"It's so good!" She says between bites.

"Thanks, I knew you'd like it." I grin, putting my hand on her leg and I feel her stiffen.

"Kaleb," She tries to push me away, "You're distracting me."

"That was the plan." I say cockily with a smirk, as I run my hand up and down her inner thigh. I keep moving up and down, but not it's close enough as she shuffles towards me.

Soon I can't wait any longer, "Want seconds?"

She shakes her head as she bites her bottom lip, unable to answer.

"How about dessert?" My hand travels up to her

pussy, all the way this time and I feel the warmth radiating from between her legs through the scrap of material she considers underwear.

She nods slowly.

"Good."

Serena

Kaleb takes the dishes out to the kitchen before returning with another bottle of wine. He pours me a glass never breaking eye contact and I squirm in my seat a little. I'm so wet right now, I can feel my thong clinging to my damp skin.

His apartment is gorgeous, he's filled it with candles and soft music but I'd be lying if I said I wasn't getting a little impatient. We haven't been intimate since the other day and I miss the feel of him, the way he smells. I *need* him and each day it gets worse. I rub my legs together, trying and failing to casually unstick my panties. He laughs as he realizes what I'm doing and takes a sip of his wine. I'm blushing now and my skin feels like it's on fire.

"Take them off." He commands and I want to but for some reason I feel shy. In the office we'd still been partially dressed. Even at the party we'd both been wearing clothes so for some reason taking my knickers off now makes me feel vulnerable.

"Would you like me to help?" He asks, looking at me with a mischievous glint in his eye.

I say nothing as he pushes my chair out before getting onto his knees before me. It reminds me of when he rubbed my feet in the store a few weeks ago. He slides his hands up my legs, we both watch absorbed in the movement as they slip over my thighs and underneath my dress. His fingers brush against me and I swear I'm almost ready to come. It's like my body is always on the verge whenever I'm with him and it's just waiting for me to take that jump. I bite down on my bottom lip as he slides a finger inside my panties and run his fingertips up and down my slit, swirling the juices that are dripping out of me. I groan and shift in my seat as he smiles. My hand grasps at the tablecloth, clenching it my fist as he finally sinks two fingers into me while his thumb grazes my clit.

"Should I make you come right here?" He asks, as he scratches his chin with his free hand. It's like he's pondering the question, when I just want to scream at him.

"Yes!" I reply. The word comes out louder than I intended as I move my hips so that his fingers go deeper.

His thumb begins to move slowly, tracing circles

around my clit, every now and again brushing directly over the sensitive nub. He pumps his fingers in and out of me to a similar rhythm and in that moment I want to call Kaleb a god. He leans up and kisses me, his mouth gentle against mine as he works my lips open further, deepening our embrace. With his free hand he pulls me closer and finger fucks me faster until everything is a blur. I can't stop my orgasm as it builds, every touch winding me tighter and tighter until my body is no longer under my control. I twitch in his hand, desperate to reach the finish line. I pull away from his kiss and suddenly it's like a burst of light behind my eyelids as my whole body shudders. I can feel my pussy clenching around his fingers, wanting more as I come. As I ride out the ripples he slowly withdraws his fingers and hooks them in the waistband of my panties before pulling them down and placing them on the table in front of me. We both wordlessly look at the scrap of fabric; it is now two different shades of red where the evidence of my lust has soaked through. Kaleb winks at me as he stands and offers me his hand.

"Would you like seconds of dessert?" He asks and I look up at him.

"Yes. God yes." I practically beg.

KALEB

Serena's flushed from her orgasm and I know that now is the perfect time. Taking her by the hand, I lead her up the stairs to my master bedroom. I'm going to make love to her until she can't remember her own name.

"Candles here too? Nice touch." She says quietly as she looks around taking in the black silk bed sheets and mahogany furniture.

I pull her closer to me, "I'm glad you approve." I kiss her lightly, tasting the wine on her lips. Her body fits with mine perfectly, we were made for each other. I slip my hands in her hair, pulling it loose and tug her head back gently, "You're mine, aren't you?"

"Yes," She replies breathlessly.

I grin, claiming her mouth with my own. I push her against the wall, kissing her and not holding anything back. It was raw passion. Need. I *needed* Serena like I needed air to breathe. She moans against my mouth and my dick twitches against my jeans, demanding to be free. I wanted to be inside her now. But I also wanted to take my time. I carry her to the bed and stand back to look at her. Her legs gently fall apart, showing me that bare pussy and I lick my lips. I love knowing that her soaked panties are downstairs on my dinner table. We both work quickly to pull our clothes off before I kneel between her legs and demand more hungry kisses.

"Lay back." I order and she does.

I admire her naked body before I move down, leaving a trail of kisses along her breasts, ribs, even her bellybutton gets my attention before I stop just below her hips. I part her legs further before leaning down to softly taste her. My tongue teasing, she squirms as I hold on to her thighs. I feel Serena lose herself as I torture her, not quite giving her what she wants as she bucks against me. I will never get enough of this I think as I eat her pussy like it is the best dessert ever. I will never get enough of her.

I tug on her clit with my teeth making her groan before I slide my mouth down to her opening. As I push my tongue inside her, I feel hands fisting in my hair pulling me closer. Tonight is all about her as she starts repeating my name with each raspy breath. My tongue fucks her now in slow motions as she pushes herself onto my face.

"Oh." She cries and I know she wants release, I can feel it but I don't give into her.

She whimpers as I flick lightly on her clit and she can't keep still anymore as her body begins to convulse and grind against me. She's so wet, practically dripping, and I know she must be throbbing by now so when she pulls on my hair again, I don't deny her. Eating her pussy like I was a starving man, I fuck her with my mouth until her legs close around my head. She gets closer and closer as my tongue moves faster, until finally she cries out and I take all she has. It's such a turn on seeing her at my mercy.

After giving her one last leisurely lick, tasting her gets me drunker than the wine, I move up her body. Her eyes are half closed and as she comes back from the high, I'm not finished with her. I squeeze her tits, my tongue flicking over each pebbled nipple in turn as she offers herself to me in response. I lick, suck and pull until she's moaning beneath me again. Her legs wrap around me as she tries to pull me closer, my cock at her entrance.

"Look at me." I tell her and her beautiful eyes look back into mine, this moment is everything. "I want you to know that *I love you* more than anything and I want you Serena. Always."

Her eyes widen, she clearly wasn't expecting me to

tell her I that I loved her again. I know she feels the same way, I just don't know if she'll say it tonight. She wiggles her hips against me, breaking the moment and gasps as my dick pushes its way into her slick pussy.

"Oh God." She moans pulling me closer.

We move slowly at first, stretching her as I continue playing with her breasts and she drags her nails down my back. Soon we're in a frenzy; each thrust intensified. Each time Serena cries out, I want to come.

"Look at me." I demand as she starts to close her eyes. Serena nods, and I can't help but feel lucky to have her back in my life. Right now she looks beyond fucking unbelievably beautiful. Her wavy hair is now messy and her lips now swollen and pink as her face changes each time my cock hits the right spot. Her tits bounce with every thrust and I resist the urge to reach down and bite her nipple as I fuck her. Her pussy tightens around me and I know that she's on the verge of her third orgasm of the night.

"Kaleb…" Her nails dig into my shoulders as she says my name over and over again, almost like a plea.

"Yes. Come baby." I tell her as her back arches off the bed, the orgasm taking over her body, "Come on my cock Serena. Come all over it."

"Oh fuck." She says and I can feel her nails break the skin on my back but I don't care.

"Mmmm, you taste so delicious." I say as I take another kiss from her. My cock hardens even more if that's possible.

With every thrust of my hips I can feel my dick going deeper until it feels like I'm at her very core. I fuck her faster as we look into each other's eyes; we're so lost in one another that when she comes I do too. Her orgasm pushes me over the edge as her cunt clamps around me. This isn't just fucking, I'm loving her with everything I have. I'm giving her my all.

Serena

I splay my fingers out across his chest, my cheek resting on his bare skin. I can hear his heart beating steadily, drumming out a beat I already know. He lets out a snore and pulls me tighter to him. I relish moments like this. I live for them. Sean's away and I can be here with Kaleb finally, guilt free. Well almost guilt free, I owe Sean honesty but Kaleb is so entwined in my head and heart that saying goodbye is impossible. I can't cut him out, because it would be like gouging out chunks of myself. I'm not ready to be mutilated and broken. And leaving Kaleb would break me.

I turn away onto my side, the tendrils of guilt that crept in are now holding me firmly. Doubts and worries come crashing down and I struggle to breathe. I want Kaleb, I need him but I promised Sean forever. My head starts to thump and I can feel a headache coming on.

My family loves Sean, he loves me, he is who I

should be with but every time I leave Kaleb it's harder to go home. I'm a whore. A mess. A greedy, selfish person who is afraid of the repercussions no matter which man I choose. And suddenly my chest begins to hurt and I can't breathe. Is my heart breaking? I. Can't. Breathe. I'm a bad person. A tear threatens to escape.

I

Can't.

Breathe.

An arm wraps around my waist and Kaleb moves closer to me, his chest against my back. The warmth of his body spreads through me as his legs weave through mine. He calms me. He grounds me and my body relaxes. I must be fucking crazy to think that I should give this up for Sean and my family. Without him I can't breathe. This life is slowly suffocating me, the wedding, the plans to pop out a baby, heck even the new house makes my skin itch. It has done from the beginning, but I ignored all those feelings. Once upon a time I thought Sean was everything I wanted, he was faithful, devoted and hardworking. I was convinced that he wouldn't break my heart. But lately he's been different. He's changed and I'm only now starting to see that. He drinks way too much, puts me down and tries to control everything I do. I don't love him, not the way I should. I can't force feelings for him and I'm done trying. With Kaleb everything just *is*. It comes naturally. His lips gently kiss my shoulder.

"Are you okay?" He whispers in the darkness.

"Yeah." I say, pulling his arm tighter around me. We lay in silence for a moment.

I ask him, "Do you think I'm a bad person?"

"What?"

"For doing this to Sean. For hurting him." I voice my thoughts; I need to know what Kaleb thinks. I have to talk about how I feel because I can feel it building, and soon my cup will run over.

He strokes my hair as he talks and I can feel the vibrations from his chest against my body.

"No one is perfect Serena, not even Sean. Should we have done this properly? Yes— because I love you and I want to be with you. Only you. But we didn't and now we have to live with that."

I whisper as he falls silent, "That didn't answer my question…"

Kaleb pulls me closer like he's afraid I'm going to pick Sean and leave him. "You're only human, and you've made a mistake. That doesn't make you a horrible person, just a conflicted one."

KALEB

I hate seeing Serena feel guilty about being with me behind Sean's back and I wish I could tell her the truth. She needs to know that Sean is a piece of shit, a scumbag and that she deserves better. I want to tell her. But I can't. How can I tell her that he knows about us being together and he doesn't really give a damn as long as I keep bailing him out? The only thing he cares about is his own selfish ass. As long as he's got cash and someone to warm his bed, he doesn't give a shit about her. *Fuck* that makes me angry because she has to *know* but I'm not ready to tell her everything, not when I've only just got her to myself.

I comfort her the best way I can, telling her that she's not a horrible person and it's true, she's not. If anyone is horrible it's me for lying. I try not to focus on that right now. We don't have a lot of time together this weekend and I want to make the most of it. She drifts back to sleep with her head on my chest and we both stay wrapped up in each other until almost 10am. Later I make us breakfast and we chat like a normal couple would. I find myself wanting this every day.

"How is your family doing?" I ask.

She brightens up when she talks about her family; I know how important they are to her.

She takes a sip of her coffee, "They're good, I haven't seen them much lately but I plan to soon. What about your mum? Does she still work at the salon?"

I nod, "Yes, she called me the other day and said she wanted me to visit for Christmas," I pause before I decide to tell her exactly what my mother said. Serena is eating her scrambled eggs as she eyes me, looking like she's just been thoroughly fucked, which she had, "She wants you to come."

Serena drops the fork and covers her mouth with both hands.

I chuckle, "It's OK, I probably won't get to see her anyway but she suspects I'm seeing someone. She's like a dog with a bone when she thinks I'm keeping something from her."

Her hands move, "Wow, I mean – I don't know what to say."

I smile and I know it doesn't reach my eyes because I would give anything to have Serena in my life as my official girlfriend and more. She takes a drink and looks down at her food, and I know that I've ruined our moment. That was the last thing I wanted to do.

"Serena, my mother is meddlesome and I haven't seen her much lately so she gets nosy when I don't visit." I want to reassure her that there's no pressure. I need her to know that I'm not trying to force her to make a decision right now and run away with me.

She nods, "Mine is like that sometimes too."

I change the subject and we finish breakfast but I can't help wonder what it would be like for her to meet my family officially because I just know they'd love her too.

Serena gets dressed and starts gathering up her things. She's almost set to leave now and this is the part I hate the most, I fucking hate it. She goes to put her panties in her bag but I place my hand over hers and take them from her. I slip them into my pocket and smile at her.

"These are mine now." I say as I kiss the top of her head. She just grins at me and puts her shoes on.

"I'm going to miss this." I know that I'm hinting at something here but I just can't help myself, I'm a selfish person. I know that I've laid on the guilt and I shouldn't have, but when she puts on her jacket I feel like my heart is going to stop beating at any second. I want to keep her here with me. I want to tell her everything to free her from that asshole of a 'future husband' but I can't.

She sighs happily as she rests her cheek on my hand and I pull her close. She looks content, whole. She has this glow about her and I love that I contributed to that. Deep down inside, I knew all along that she was made for me but when I left years ago, I had been blind. *She would've picked me.* I know she would have.

I kiss her then, taking her breath away and we hold onto each other like no one else exists.

Serena

I left Kaleb's last weekend and it nearly killed me, I wanted to go back again but Kaleb was busy and I'd already made plans with Laura to scope out whoever's been stealing my money even though I think deep down I know. My mind is all over the place but as I'm at Laura's house watching her tuck in her daughter, Daisy, I realize that the best things in life are never easy. She gives her a kiss on the forehead and pulls the covers up as they whisper their 'I love yous'. A small part of me wants this family life that she has, nice house, gorgeous kid. Don't get me wrong, she's had to fight for it, she works harder than anyone I know but when I see her smile I know she thinks it's worth it. I frown because a few weeks ago it was everything I didn't want but now Kaleb is back in my life I feel like I have a partner, someone to do this with.

She closes the bedroom door softly behind her and grins at me, tonight we're going out. We're heading downtown to The Den, and the rush of excitement that Laura's feeling about catching the 'baddies' hasn't hit me yet, this week has been a long and confusing one. After spending the weekend at Kaleb's I was now sure that I wanted to be with him, he was my happily forever after. I just needed to end it with Sean, which was proving hard because he was never home. Every time I came in from work he was leaving, and when he came home he was usually drunk so I'd just leave it. I was dreading having to tell my mother, a lump forming in my throat just thinking about it. But she would just have to wait— tonight we were hunting *baddies.*

I'm wearing a simple black dress, a pair of knee high boots and some chunky gold jewelry— I didn't want to look out of place and we didn't know how long we'd be out. Laura looked glamorous as always in a red low cut chiffon blouse and a pair of leather-look skinny jeans, no 'mom bod' as she called it in sight. She definitely didn't look like any of the mums I knew.

The Den was pretty full when we got there; it was a Sunday night so I was a little surprised. Even more surprising however, was the number of attractive men in suits that sat at the tables. I always imagined gambling to be for greasy losers in loud flowery shirts.

The bar itself was also surprisingly chic with its red brick decor, comfy leather armchairs all slightly mismatched and large gold framed mirrors that hung on every wall. If I wasn't here to find a thief I'd be tempted to order in a drink and relax, it was my kind of chilled out place.

There's some non-descript music with a steady beat playing in the background and I feel calm, calmer than I thought I would. We order two cocktails, and they arrive brightly colored and with a wedge of lime on the glass. Laura said we should just sit and wait, but after my second drink I was getting restless. It turns out I'm not the only one as Laura leans over the bar to talk to the middle aged barman, he looks tired and worn down.

"Hey, we're looking for someone." She shouts over the beat and the crowd that's starting to grow as the place gets busier.

"Can't help you." He replies flatly, not even looking up from the whiskey he's pouring, on the rocks.

She waves a hand in front of his face trying to get his attention, "Come on... someone who comes in every other weekend roughly and spends about two thousand a time. Might come in on the odd night during the week but only spends a couple of hundred."

The man looks up, "Actually...yeah I know him" He lets out a small chuckle as he looks us up and down, "Sean left you by the wayside too huh? He's good at that."

I straighten at the mention of his name, sure I heard wrong. "Did you just say Sean?"

"Look ladies, I'm sorry he's blown you off or given you the wrong number but you only have yourself to blame, he's our resident playboy."

"Sean? A playboy?" Laura snorts before avoiding my glare by taking a sip of her drink.

"Different girl on his arm every time he comes in here. Says it brings him luck." The guy shrugs as if it's nothing.

I pull out my phone and show the bartender my screensaver, a picture of Sean I took on our trip to New York last winter, "This guy?"

"Yeah. Sean." There's a bored tone to his voice now, he's obviously had women come looking for my fiancé before.

"Maybe he didn't *do* anything with those women. Maybe they just...blow on the dice and go home alone?" Laura adds, trying to find a positive but I give her another glare and it's the bartenders turn to snort.

I guess we've discovered who has been taking my money and what they've been spending it on. My mind is reeling and I can't make it stop. How many times? How many lies? Did this make us even? No. He was sleeping with multiple strangers. I was with Kaleb. I loved Kaleb— that had to count for something. But Sean? Sean. Good, dependable, *loyal*, Sean. No. He hasn't been any of those things for a long time— that wasn't right. Drunk, abusive, cheating, stealing Sean.

How the fuck has he been able to afford to put it back?

KALEB

There's a lot on my mind this week. Serena and I had more than an amazing time together last weekend and I wish that I could wake up with her by my side every day. Damn, at this point I don't want to keep lying to her anymore. I used to tell myself it's for her own good but the deeper we go, the more damage I do. I know Sean isn't loyal to her, he steals from her and I tried to help him but I failed. All I ever wanted was for Serena to be happy and now she can be… *with me.* For that to happen she needs to know the truth but if she did, would she stay? If it came from me, would she forgive me? Would she hate me? I just don't know.

There are a lot of unknowns at the moment and that's stressing me the fuck out. I know I can get this situation under my control I just need to take a deep breath. Sean was a speckle in the grand scheme of things and after he was out of the picture, Serena and I could be happy.

I know I'm getting ahead of myself as I think about planning a vacation for us together. Even though Serena doesn't do flashy, I want the best of the best for her. So I go online and look at the different places we could go, I think carefully about the things she likes and doesn't. As I browse, I wonder what would have happened if I'd never helped Sean to begin with? He seemed to spiral deeper and deeper down, lying and gambling more as he started to take out his frustrations and anger on Serena. I watched him become a nasty, twisted son of a bitch. *What would have become of Serena if I hadn't come back?*

I had a feeling, if I hadn't left years ago, we would be married by now, hell she'd be pregnant if we didn't already have a kid. I'd be taking care of her and she'd be my wife and we would've never had to deal with all this shit in the first place. But instead...

After a while of looking through different locations, I finally find something that I know she'll love. It's luxurious and simple at the same time— but I know that Serena won't be able to travel anywhere with me until she breaks things off with Sean. For that to happen she'd have to know everything.

I book the entire vacation for two months' out anyway and hope that by then I'll have figured it out. Meanwhile, I have a lot to do to put everything in place. The first thing is to cut Sean off and make sure that he never takes a penny from Serena's account again. Next, I need to convince her to move in with me. The guilt is eating at me, no doubt but I have to try to do whatever I can to keep her this time around. Even if I seem like I'm crazy for doing everything I have.

Serena

"Come on, let's go home..." Laura says as I down another shot of tequila. I begged her to stay out at the bar with me, I don't know why but somewhere in the back of my mind I was hoping that Sean would walk in and I could confront him. The drunker I got, the angrier I became. Then I felt guilty, how did I have any right to be angry with him? I was cheating too; our relationship was shambles.

But I was going to leave him and he planned to keep stringing me along, robbing me, using me and wearing me down. The more time I spend with Kaleb, the more I realize how Sean has been playing me, emotionally crippling me by putting me down and making me into a shell of my former self. I cheated with Kaleb before, and I stayed when I should have left but since then all Sean has done is hollow me out and made me pay a thousand times over.

I want to feel something. I want to feel alive and

Kaleb does that. Every touch makes me feel something electric, like my body is becoming mine again. Suddenly the tequila isn't enough, drowning my sorrows isn't going to work no matter how supportive Laura is being. It's like she knows what I'm thinking as she rubs my back and soothingly says my nickname over and over again.

"It's okay Rena, it'll work out I promise."

"I want to go…I need…Kaleb." I say, and she smiles knowingly. Laura isn't so lucky with love herself, her deadbeat ex-boyfriend was a drug addict who bailed the second those blue lines appeared and Daisy came into being, but she was a hopeless romantic. Plus she hated Sean, so Kaleb was a huge step up in her books.

"I'll call you a cab and I'll get you there quicker than you can lick that salt off your sticky hand, which by the way is vile, we're not 21 anymore Rena – tequila is for college students." I know she's trying to take my mind off Sean but I don't even smile at that comment.

She digs my phone out of my bag and calls a taxi, and then she fires off a quick text to Kaleb to let him know I'm coming. She's true to her word and I'm standing outside his house, in front of his door before I can even order another round of shots.

Tonight I need Kaleb in a way that I can't describe; I need to feel him inside me. I need him. The second it opens, only a crack, I push it and close it quickly behind us. I place my hands on his face and bring his lips down to meet mine. I don't want words right now, I want to *feel*. My fingers make light work of his shirt buttons as I practically tear it open and push it down over his arms and fling it to the floor. His lips break into a smile against my mouth, and he breathes "Hey, what's the rush tiger?" before kissing me again.

My hands slide over his chest tracing the patterns of his ink without looking— that's how well I know his body. I pull away to look at him, just for a moment. My lips pressing gently against the tattoo on his shoulder before my hands move lower.

"No talking." I command as I slide my fingers through his belt loops and pull him closer to me.

I struggle for a moment to unbuckle his belt and pull it off, before throwing that to the floor too. Pushing his trousers down over his hips I smile when I realize he isn't wearing any boxers. I raise an eyebrow at him and he shrugs at me grinning.

I lower myself down onto my knees and his eyes practically light up when he realizes what I'm about to do. All thoughts of Sean and what he's done vanish completely from my mind as Kaleb's cock twitches in front of my face, begging to be touched. Every sense that should be dulled by the alcohol is in fact heightened, my whole body has been set alight and I need to relieve some of the pressure that's building.

I wrap my hand around his dick and slowly begin to massage him. I use my free hand to cup his balls and when he lets out a feral groan I'm hornier than I ever thought I would be. A small bead of pre-cum forms on the head of his cock and without thinking about it, without feeling self-conscious, my tongue flicks out to taste him. The look in his eyes as he watches makes me want to give him more, and I take him in my mouth. As my head starts to bob up and down he weaves his hands through my hair, pulling me deeper onto him. His taste is addictive, slightly salty and strangely sweet. I imagine I appear like I'm gorging on him like an all you can eat buffet when he takes a sharp intake of breath and his body tightens. I move quicker, paying special attention to the head of his cock, sucking in as I move to increase the pressure and it's only seconds before my enthusiastic sucking pays off. Kaleb holds me still as his cum coats the back of my throat and he moans with satisfaction. Pulling away I lick my lips, stand up and slide off my dress. The night has just begun and I'm only getting started. Tonight I need him to fuck any guilt, any thoughts of Sean and anything else that tries to interrupt out of my head. Tonight I only want to focus on feeling.

KALEB

My phone goes off early in the morning, the vibrating noise like a drill in my head. Serena moves to stretch but a soft snore tells me she's not awake yet. I'm not really surprised after last night, drunk and horny Serena is someone I could get used to. I grin to myself as I get up, grab my cell phone and step out of the room.

"What?" I answer, pissed off because it's Sean, of course.

"She's with you, isn't she?" He sounds drunk as usual. Who the hell is drunk at 6 am?

I walk into the living room and look the window, checking to see that he isn't waiting somewhere outside. It's the type of psycho move he'd pull when he's been hitting the bottle.

"What do you want Sean?" I ask avoiding the question. Not like he doesn't know where she is. He left her alone again. He's off spending her cash and fucking some other woman but he acts like he's the innocent party.

He chuckles, "Wow, not even fucking your car up teaches you a lesson. What do I have to do—"

"It was you?" Am I really surprised?

He laughs harder this time, and it's sinister, "Who else would it be?"

"You shouldn't have done that." I say in a flat tone. I don't want to threaten him, he's drunk and I don't know how he'll react. I also don't want to fuel his fire by giving him a reaction either.

Sean shakes it off as a game, "What are you going to do exactly?" He challenges.

I don't answer right away and Sean thinks he has me where he wants me.

"Nothing, because you know you can't. So you're going to stay away from Serena or next time it won't be your *car*."

"There won't be a next time." I say through gritted teeth because honestly, it's getting easier and easier for him to get to me.

There's a silence for a second on the other side, "Sure and while you're on the phone I need you to do another money transfer—"

"Are you fucking serious? Do you think I'm just going to keep covering your gambling ass? Why would I?" My voice rising as the conversation goes on. My fist tightens and I feel my control slipping, "She doesn't even want to be with you anymore." I let it slip before I have a chance to think anything through.

"She comes home to me and that's how I know she'll always choose me." I could practically see his smug face and if he'd been standing in front of me, I'd rearrange his facial features without a second thought.

The line goes dead after that and now I'm left with words I want to say that I've been holding back for a very long time. The prick thinks Serena loves him! *Is he crazy?* He's been fucking her over for far too long. She knows what he's like, her eyes have been opened and there's no going back now.

"Motherfucker." I hiss, only it's too late now, there's no one on the other end.

"Kaleb?" I jump as I hear her voice coming from the kitchen and I turn to find her wearing my t-shirt and a confused look on her face. Fuck, I hope she didn't hear anything. I'm losing control and I can't tell her now, not like this. I need to get everything straight. I have to be calm.

"Who was that?" Her eyes search mine for answers and in that moment I really want to tell her everything but I'm too worked up to even think straight.

"I have to go to the office." I say briskly instead and leave to get changed.

She tries to touch me as I walk past her but I feel dirty, I feel like everything is slipping away and right now I don't deserve her love. It would make me feel worse than I already did.

"Kaleb, talk to me." Serena follows me into the room.

I sigh and take a deep breath trying to soothe the anger that's building inside, but it's not towards her. "I promise to explain everything to you tonight. Make yourself at home and tonight we'll talk."

She seems hesitant but she nods slowly, "Fine, we'll talk tonight."

I was relieved but it was only temporary. After showering and changing quickly, I leave Serena drinking coffee in the kitchen. She's quiet but she doesn't ask any more questions. And now I know that I have to tell her everything tonight. I don't know how I'm going to do it. How do I say the words? Does it even matter now?

After she learns the truth she's going to run for the hills or even worse, stay with Sean out of that misplaced guilt she has. She's only just started to realize who he is but she could end up going backwards. She could argue that he's sick and needs some serious help; he's got this whole sob story/addiction thing going on. But me? She'll never forgive me. No. I'd lose her now but I wasn't about to let her go so easily. She'd sit and listen to everything I had to say and after that she could make her decision. At least that was the way I was hoping tonight would go.

Serena

I woke with more of a sex hangover than an actual one, my body ached and was stretched in ways I didn't think it could be but I was happy. I was going to come clean with Sean as soon as I got home and I was going to kick him out— it was my home after all. I rolled over and reached out across to Kaleb's side only to be met with warm bed sheets, he was gone. He must have just gotten up.

I hear a low voice and I relax as I realize he's in the kitchen, probably on the phone resolving some work issue. I grab a t-shirt from his drawer and throw it on, he sounds angry now and I wonder what the matter is. I quietly open the door a crack so as not to disturb him and I freeze. What had I just walked into? The conversation Kaleb was having on the phone…No.

It couldn't have been what I thought it was, except I wasn't sure. I'd caught the last part of the conversation about gambling and a woman, they were talking about a woman. Was it *me*? Could it have been Sean on the end of the call? But that didn't make sense.

I was in a state of denial as Kaleb got dressed and left saying there was a work emergency, but the way he shied away from my touch made my mind scream out that something was wrong. He asked me to stay put today and said that we'd talk when he came home and I agreed because I didn't know what else to do. Grabbing a pair of shorts from his cupboard I pulled them on; I didn't want to wear my little black dress because the faint smell of booze was making my stomach churn.

I lasted about an hour pacing around his apartment before I decided to do some digging and find out what he was hiding. I wasn't sure what I was looking for but Kaleb was acting strange and after everything I'd been through with Sean I didn't want any more secrets.

Snooping wasn't something I wanted to do, I wanted to trust him but I couldn't get this niggle out of my head that something was very wrong. If I was going to give us a shot, I had to know. I looked around his office/spare room and could have smiled. Kaleb was organized, he had labelled folders stacked inside his desk drawers making it easy to have a rifle through but I didn't see anything out of the ordinary.

My gut feeling was failing me as I searched in the kitchen drawers and only found one that contained his bill receipts.

I was about to give up until I remembered to check his bedroom too. This was crappy of me, I knew it but I couldn't shake the feeling that something wasn't quite right. What I heard Kaleb say, his reaction after he saw me and how he left— avoiding my touch and then telling me he wanted to talk later was just too much to ignore.

All I found in his dresser were neatly folded clothes, no paperwork of any kind. No suspicious pictures, no dodgy second phone. Nothing. I looked in his closet but it was the same, just clothes. Moving to his bedside table I pull open the drawers, my heartbeat hammering in my ears and I knew before I found anything that this was it. This is the line I cannot uncross.

The first one I checked had his address book, planner and some other miscellaneous things. The second drawer down contained a folder marked 'Bank Statements' and I clumsily took the papers out of the file and looked them over. The latest transactions seemed to be normal, except…he'd withdrawn a large amount of money. The amount mirrored exactly what had been taken out of *my* account and put back in days later, down to the cent. I tipped the file out onto the bed and I went through each sheet until I found exactly what I was looking for. Kaleb had a years' worth of statements in that file, and each month there was at least one, if not more transactions that I knew matched up to mine. I knew it because I'd spent hours agonizing over where my money was going. This was only for the past year though, how long had this been going on?

My mobile pinged, and I saw a text from Laura, 'Who's the blonde lady Sean is with? He's heading towards the house!'

Sean was fucking some whore in my house, in my bed and Kaleb...well Kaleb was helping him. Kaleb deceived me and played me just like Sean had. I was a fool, a fucking fool but no longer.

It ended today.

KALEB

I'm done with Sean. I decided it last night when Serena had shown up, she was drunk and she wanted me. Me. So this morning when he rung I made sure the phone recorded the entire conversation. I needed to rip his perfect mask off and show the world what a scumbag he was. He obviously had a death wish. My hands tighten around the steering wheel as I head to the police station and growl in frustration.

I listen to the recording over and over again, it makes my blood boil each time. It's my breaking point; the way he thinks he can still claim Serena as his. I'm so mad at myself for letting it get this far that I can't see straight. All the time I wasted trying to help him get his shit together, but he was never going to be worthy of her and I'm done covering his ass, even if that means Serena learns everything. At this point I don't see it ending any other way. She has to know who has been there for her this entire time.

I don't know if she'll forgive me but either way, I put my feelings aside because this is not just about me, it's about her. I'm telling Serena everything tonight but first I needed to make sure the cops knew about what Sean did to my car. Granted, that wasn't as terrible as I wanted it to be but the stealing was.

I stopped off at the bank on my way and grabbed extra copies of my bank statements, I'd stupidly left mine back at my house and I didn't want to face Serena until this was done. Sean was going to go down for blackmailing and stealing. We'd see what he had to say about that.

I should've done it sooner but I couldn't. The way he spoke to me earlier just reinforced the fact that this needed to end. He always thought that he had some power over me but it wasn't so, it was Serena who had power and now that I had her, he had nothing.

I take a couple of deep breaths to calm myself before I barge into the police station like I've lost my mind. I need to be calm and collected when the officers question me and take my statement about why I've let him blackmail me. Now I just hoped Serena wouldn't stand up for him when they questioned her too because they would. By that point though, she'd know everything. Would she defend Sean?

No, she couldn't. I hoped she didn't decide to

stick with him now, not after everything we shared and everything else we still had between us. She had seen his ugly side and she had to know what I'd done for her.

I'd told her that I loved her and meant it, but was it enough for her to forgive what I've done?

Serena

I'm on autopilot as I head back to our house. The house I bought, with the money I'd been left from my grandparents. Sean had been stealing from me, taking my money for gambling. And Kaleb knew. Did Kaleb know about all the women too? Did he know that Sean would throw my money away and drown his sorrows with a different woman every time? I feel like someone's tearing at my insides.

The cheating doesn't hurt like the lying does; after all I was hardly innocent in that department. I was trying to make this work. For years I'd been trying, doing what he wanted, dressing how he liked, and making an effort with his friends. I made fucking artichoke soup for Christ sake!

I put my key in the front door and wait, I can hear giggling coming from our bedroom and I know Sean isn't home alone. I know it, I knew it when I got Laura's text but I'm still in a state of denial. Why?

Surely this means we're even? I creep up the stairs to our bedroom. I can hear soft moans broken up with the occasional whispered word and a small laugh. Why am I doing this? I have to see for myself, I have to confirm it with my own eyes. It's the final nail in the coffin of our relationship; the blindfold has truly fallen away.

I open the door and see him, shagging her from behind, his pale ass greeting me. It's the blonde checkout girl from the bloody market, I realize as she turns to look at me. No wonder we always went there. It's like he was taunting me the whole time. Sean moves quickly, throwing a blanket to cover her and standing before me.

"Get out, you piece of shit." I say quietly

"Me?" He says with an incredulous tone. "What about you and Kaleb? Did you have to fuck him to get your promotion Serena?"

"Get out!" I say again, louder this time.

He pulls on a pair of boxers and stands before me with his hands on his hips, "It's my house too. I'm not leaving."

"What money did you use to pay for it Sean, because it sure as shit wasn't your own." I scream as I grab the closest thing to hand, a lamp, and throw it at him. He pauses briefly as it shatters against the wall behind him; he knows he'll have a fight on his hands to prove he contributed to the cost of this place, especially since he was already siphoning off me.

"I paid towards it Serena, I have shares. I have rights." The blonde has thrown on her checkout uniform hastily and is creeping past us to the door.

"Yeah okay, and where did you get that money Sean? You won it." I'm screaming now and I can't stop. "You won it using my money to place the fucking bets!"

"If you'd been here… If you'd loved me like you love him!" He spat out as he takes a step towards me. He grunts with anger as he swipes his arm across my dressing table throwing the contents to the floor. Bottles smash, the mixed scents rise up and make me gag as glass crunches under his feet as he moves closer again.

I'm done shying away and I dig my finger into his chest, stabbing at him with each word that flows from my mouth. There's no off switch now. "Don't you dare! I gave you everything, every last ounce of me and it was never enough. So this is all just revenge? Is that it?"

He takes another step forward and I'm backed

against the wall, "No." He growled, "I realized I was losing…"

"Control, Sean. You weren't worried about losing me, you were worried about losing control *of* me. There's a big difference." My voice is lowered, it's like I've run out of fight. We both have.

His shoulders slump and he knows that we'll never go back from this point. What we had, in its false perfection, the ideal life he was building is nothing but a ruin. The trashed room, with its smashed lights, the crumpled dirty bed sheets soaked with his sins and the glass, fragmented and saturating the room with a smell I'll never forget and then it hits me, this moment will forever be seared into my brain— the end of us.

"Get.The.Fuck.Out." I whisper, looking away from the man I'd been with since I was eighteen.

"Fine." He grinds out. He bundles up the rest of his clothes from the floor and leaves, slamming the front door behind him. I look out the window as he climbs into his car with her, he catches me watching and just grins. He's still trying to find a way under my skin but I'm past that now.

The sun sets and I'm still standing at the damn window, I haven't been able to make myself move. I feel an ache in my chest, but I don't think it's for

Sean. In fact, I'm relieved that he's gone. It stings a little, I did love him once but now I wasn't filled with guilt over my feelings for Kaleb. Kaleb. How much did Kaleb know? That's the thought that keeps going round my head. I need to know. I'm having a shit day, and I don't want any more lies. I can't take any more.

I want answers.

So I call a cab and head straight for the store. I find him still in his office, a frown on his face, as he looks at all the line counts in front of him. He stands as I enter.

"Serena? What are you doing here? I was just on my way back to you now." He looks at my mascara running down my face, my crumpled clothes and tries to pull me into a hug. "What happened? Are you okay?"

The genuine warmth in his voice is making me feel like breaking, I want to fold into him and have him hold me while I cry out all my misery. But he is part of my anguish. How can I still want him as much as I do?

"Don't lie to me Kaleb. Did you know about the women?" I'm direct. I came here for answers.

"Yes." He looks away, ashamed. That's all it takes and my calmness dissolves into a world of lies.

"*You knew!*" I screamed, pushing him away. "You

knew Sean was cheating on me, gambling my money away and you. Never. Said. A. Fucking. Thing." I hit his chest with my fists, wanting him to feel my pain. They had both betrayed me.

Taking a step back so I was out of his reach, I say nothing as Kaleb runs a hand through his hair. I can see the hurt on his face but he has caused this. He let me live with these lies.

"What was I supposed to do?" He asked, shrugging, "I was going to tell you…"

"Be honest with me? Heck, I don't know, tell me before all this started! I thought you loved me." I was sobbing now. Both of the men in my life were liars. Did I not mean anything to them?

"That's why I left! Who do you think paid your bills? Who do you think bailed Sean out, again and again Serena? Me! If that wasn't me loving you, I don't know what is."

Through broken sobs I managed to rasp "W-w-what?"

"Your mother convinced me that I'd never be good enough for you. A casual fling she called me. She said that you were getting it all out of your system before you married the love of your life, Sean. Good old dependable, grown up Sean— except he wasn't." He sounds bitter now.

My mind is reeling; nothing is what I thought it was. No one is who I thought they were. "How did my mother know?" I whisper.

Kaleb sits on the edge of his desk, looking down at his hands, "Sean always knew about the affair, I guess he must have told her."

"If he knew, why didn't he confront me? Why didn't he say anything?" Tears stream down my cheeks as I try to process Kaleb's words.

"If he had he knew there was a chance he'd lose you. You're smart, beautiful and if he came and told you he knew…you might have chosen me."

Would I have chosen Kaleb? Yes, a part of me would have. The last few years my life had become stale, it was slow and most days were a numb struggle. I was always waiting for something more, wanting something exciting and Kaleb was that for me. I'd tried to convince myself I was working towards my dream life, but my dreams had changed even before I'd met Kaleb. Sean and I had been drifting along before our affair.

"But that doesn't explain why you bailed him out?" My tears have stopped and I find myself watching him intently.

"When I found out what that dick was up to I thought that it would hurt you more to lose him.

Your mother said he was the love of your life remember, plus I was always your dirty little secret. I thought being together was never an option for us." Kaleb sighs, stands and walks behind his desk. He can't seem to stay still.

"So I helped him out, I told him I was leaving and that he needed to get his shit together. He swore that he would, but people like Sean never change. They just suck you dry and walk away."

I snorted in response. I was quickly learning just how much of a douche my fiancé was. Kaleb said he didn't want to hurt me, he was trying to protect me, and save the relationship he thought I wanted. But he hurt me. What we had, was it just sex? How could he love me and lie to me? Was he going to leave again?

"You could have fought for me. You could have tried harder!" I croak out, my throat sore from fighting with Sean.

"I didn't think you wanted me Serena." Kaleb's voice is low. I want to believe that he regrets what he did, but how can I?

"You didn't give me that choice!" I can hear my voice getting louder and louder as I can barely control my anger. "You just left me! You left me and you never said anything about Sean. You let him hurt me over and over again."

"I know. I'm so sorry." But I don't hear him clearly because I've already left.

KALEB

I let her go.

The disgusted look she gave me was something I couldn't stand much longer. Serena was crushed – heartbroken and as she pointed her finger at me and yelled. I just stood there like a statue. I can't deny the things she said. There's no excuse I can give, even though I only wanted her to be happy but the thing is she wasn't. I knew she hadn't been for a long time and I did nothing about it. Instead I left her with Sean, the scumbag who wasted three years of all our lives.

I wanted to tell her that I loved her but it wasn't what she needed to hear. I wanted to tell her the truth myself and I waited so long for the right moment that she ended up finding out on her own. It was my fault, she hated me and I couldn't stop her. In the back of my mind I think about all of the time we spent together recently, those moments were *real*, more real than her relationship with Sean had ever been. What we have has always been the real deal from the very beginning. We're meant to be together and I'll never give up now. I'm older, wiser – you could say and even though I messed up, I would never do what Sean did to her. I'd even let her hate me if it made her feel better but the fact of the matter is that no one else will make her happy, not like I can.

I leave the office and go home but I can't relax. All I think about is Serena. After working out, I take a shower and then I make dinner but I don't have much of an appetite and that's when I give up. Before getting to my room so I can try to sleep, my phone vibrates on the counter. Reluctantly, I grab it and answer.

"Kaleb." At the sound of the voice I almost wish I hadn't answered, "Kaleb, are you there?" It's my mother.

"Yes." I reply and hope this conversation goes quickly.

"Hmm, you sound strange. Anyway, since you haven't called me back, I wanted to know if you were still coming home—"

"Mom..." I say in a warning tone because I know what's coming. She's going to try to guilt me and right now I really don't want to be around people.

She sighs, "I knew it! I told your father you

wouldn't come so he said we should come to you for the holidays! We've booked our plane tickets." She says excited and no matter how much I didn't want to be around anyone, I couldn't be mad at her.

"Mom, I – I guess that's ok if you really want to." I'll have to deal with my issues and get over it because I couldn't take it out on my family.

She squeals, "Perfect! We'll see you soon but I'll let you go now because I have to run some errands and start gift shopping!"

I put the phone down after that unsure of what just happened. Maybe it's not a bad idea that my family will be here for the holidays. If Serena is still upset, it would be something to keep me distracted. For now, I just lay in bed unable to fall asleep, thinking about what happens next. It could go either way. Serena would either forgive me or she would hate me forever.

What would she choose?

Serena

I'd spent the last few days curled up in my bed, not moving. I'd received one message from Kaleb saying he was pressing charges against Sean for the money, blackmail and something about a car. He said that he recommended that I do the same and that he'd already told the police about my issue. The police are going to arrest Sean at some point today or tomorrow. Then nothing. I think he was trying to give me space, but a part of me wanted him to say something, anything to fix this.

Sean must have spoken to the authorities, he must know what's about to happen because he keeps trying to phone me, he's texting me non-stop and yesterday he was even knocking on my front door. I ignore everything and everyone, feeling numb and alone.

That morning it takes me a few hours of sobbing and crying to decide that I can't stay like this. I grab my bag, ram a few changes of clothes in it and get in my car. I'm falling apart and right now I just want to go home to my family. The two-hour drive takes me to the house my parents bought when we first moved here, the area was suburban enough for peace and quiet but urban enough for a Starbucks down the road. I pull into the drive and walk right in; my mother never locked the front door in the day. Apparently it's a habit she gets from her mother back in Wales, everyone knows their neighbors so they trust each other. I love this house, it was their forever home. It had four bedrooms, a huge kitchen, even a library for my father and overlooked a golf course and a lake— I say lake but it was more of a large pond. It was the American Dream to my parents, a hard-working couple from Wales who grew up on a council estate.

My dad was in the kitchen making a cup of tea as I walk in dumping my bags on the floor. I probably look like a mess, wearing the same yoga pants and baggy t-shirt that I've worn for the last two days, I haven't showered and I don't even know where my hair brush has run off to.

"I'm here to stay for a few days." I say simply as he gives me a smile. One of the things I love about my father is that he's uncomplicated and never pushes me. It makes him the total opposite to my mother, who always has to add her two cents to every situation. Speak of the devil, she strolls in unsurprised to see me. She must have seen me pull up.

"Sean rung an hour ago to ask if you were here, he seems worried about you. Said you were having some sort of breakdown?" She looks concerned, and I feel a twinge of guilt for complaining about her. Despite her overbearing ways she does love me.

And Sean. Of course Sean's been in touch. He's been lighting my phone up like it's the 4th of July and in the end I turned it off on the drive over. Between the constant calls off him and the overwhelming silence from Kaleb I haven't got the space to think properly.

"Is this about that Kaleb man? Cariad, he's not the one for you." The way she reverts to the Welsh term of endearment tells me that she's more than a little worried, but the way she grinds out Kaleb's name reminds me that she's firmly on Sean's side.

I sigh and accept a steaming mug from my father, "Mum, I'm here because I've had enough of the both of them. They both lied to me."

"Sean wouldn't do that, he loves you." She's insistent, even until the end but she doesn't know what he's done. I don't really want to tell her but she's pushing my buttons.

I try to distance myself, to say it without crying and to my surprise it's easier today than it was yesterday. "No he doesn't, he loves my money. He loves the idea of the life he has with me."

She tilts her head at me, with that patronizing look she used to give when I was younger and I had disappointed her, "Don't say that, he sounded very worried."

The rage I'm holding in comes forth, and it's spewing out of my mouth before I can stop it. She needs to understand, she needs to know why I'm hurting so that she can back off, so that it can stop being my fault.

"That's because I'm pressing charges! He's been stealing from me! Using my money to gamble and fuck other women in our bed! Stop taking his side!" I snap.

"Ohhh Bach." My dad's arms pull me into a hug and he holds me while my mother absorbs the information I've just given her.

In her typical stern fashion she takes a deep breath and I can practically hear the cogs turning in her head as she tries to find a way to fix the mess that is my life right now.

"Well a weekend here isn't going to cut it. I think a visit to Nana is well overdue."

I look at my mother, she gives me a small smile and wraps her arms around my father and I know she only ever wanted what's best for me, but even mothers can be wrong. Sean had us all fooled. I thought I was ruining his life, but all the while he was maliciously using me. Using me like a toy he didn't want to share. He showed the world that he was the perfect husband to be, loving, caring, and hardworking but when we were alone he tore me down, hollowed me out and still wanted more.

My mother rights herself and grabs the landline phone, calling up the airport to book a flight to Wales. She gives me a thumbs up which tells me she's managed to find a flight to Cardiff. Next she rings my Grandmother or Nana as she likes to be called and tells her that I'm coming to visit. With that all sorted I take a deep breath, and go with my mug to sit out on the porch. My mum joins me after a while, wrapping an arm around my shoulder and I fall into her until my head rests against hers.

"What about Kaleb?" She asks gently.

My eyes sting and threaten to let loose the tears I've been holding back. "He knew about it, about all of it." I whisper, "I love him, but it hurts. It hurts and it's all so messy. I can't..."

She pulls me closer, "If you love him then yes, you can. You just need time."

"He's like the piece of me that was missing. When I'm with him I feel like me, I feel happy and not just existing." I try to explain, but I know how clichéd I sounded.

"I'm sorry." A sob escapes her. Her body is trembling against mine.

"Why are you sorry?" I turn to look at her, her face wet and sad.

"I should've given Kaleb a chance. I should've encouraged you to follow your heart. I just thought he was a fling..." She holds me even tighter.

"You were just doing what you thought was best, how could you know I was miserable? I didn't realize I was unhappy until him."

KALEB

She doesn't text me back. I tell her Sean will be getting arrested but she doesn't reply and she doesn't call either. I feel defeated. Like everything I wanted has just vanished with her.

"I don't know what I'm doing." I tell my mother. She phoned to talk about their visit over the holidays but she knew the second I answered that something was wrong.

She's quiet for a minute, "I never told you this but your father and I met through friends…"

"I know that."

"Kaleb, at the time we were both dating different people." She continues, as if she's unburdening herself. My family is respectable, and I can only imagine how my grandmother would have frowned on my parents' unconventional start.

"We knew nothing could come of it, so we went our separate ways and then I saw him years later. At first I couldn't stand him," She laughs as she reminisces, "But with his charming ways, he made his way through my heart."

I didn't tell my mom about what was happening with Serena, how complicated it all was with Sean, Ceci and work. However, I did tell her that I'd lost the woman I've been in love with for a very long time and I wasn't sure what to do about it. I'm like a fucking lost puppy.

"Did he mess up?" It was probably a question for my dad but I don't think it's something he'd talk about openly.

She laughs, "A lot, but I loved him and it was never something that couldn't be forgiven. We just needed our space and I needed time to think everything through. In the end, we knew we belonged together." She sighs, "Son, if she's the one for you and you're the one for her, she'll forgive you. When you know, *you know*." She says.

Shortly after, we hang up I'm still thinking about my mother's words. I never talked to her about Jen in that way, I never asked for advice. In fact, I always cringed and changed the subject when she wanted to talk about our relationship. Things were different now and I wanted her to know all about Serena. It'd been a few days and I hadn't heard from her. I made up excuses at work for her absence but…what if she doesn't come back?

I'd waited long enough. I get in the rental car and drive, I'm not sure where Serena is but I have her address so I stop by her house. There's no car outside, so I doubt she's home but I knock anyway and when no one comes to the door, I leave. There's only one other place that Serena would've gone. I hesitate when I put the key in the ignition. Serena's family doesn't like me; it's one of the reasons why I left the first time.

I put the car in reverse and make my way out of town. I remember Serena telling me where they live from before. She told me what it was like moving from Wales to America and how she loved that their new house had a porch. She couldn't believe that it had been painted a soft yellow color— she said you didn't see yellow houses back in her hometown. So although I hadn't been there before, I felt like I had. As I drive I think about how it doesn't matter who her parents like or don't. What matters is that Serena knows I'm not leaving again, I want her forever. By now, her parents must know who Sean really is. She must have told them.

The short two-hour trip feels like an eternity. She's not there, I realize when I don't see her car but I go up to the door and knock anyway. It opens and Serena's mother stands there. She looks older but she still has that same no-nonsense air about her.

"Kaleb." She says but it's not in that condescending way, like she did the last time I talked to her. No, it's almost apologetic.

I look at her questioningly but before I can even get a word out she continues.

"What I said before— I just wanted the best for her. You understand that right?" I think she means it as a rhetorical question but I nod anyway.

I'm about to turn around and go but she reaches out and catches my arm, "Kaleb she's gone, she's at the airport but you don't have long. Go and get her."

I take in her words and my heart races, "Thanks."

Quickly I get in the car and make my way to the airport. What the fuck? She can't leave, not without telling me. It's now that it hits me, what am I supposed to do if she leaves? What if she never forgives me? What if she never comes back? What if she's already on that plane?

No.

I speed, run stop signs and somehow I'm lucky because there are no cops around to stop me. Honestly I'm not even sure I would stop. My blood is pounding in my ears as the airport is in sight. Parking is fucking chaotic; I barely find a space before running inside. I look around for her but I can't see her in the waiting area, she's not getting her bags checked in either. There are a lot of people milling around, oblivious to my struggle. I hate this time of year, when everyone is trying to get somewhere for the holidays.

Then I see something. I spot her dark hair briefly. She's in the back of a line, about to board the plane. But it's through security, and I can't get to her. Not without a ticket and checking in.

"Serena!" I shout, as if my happiness depends on it— because it does.

She turns and looks around. It takes her a few moments but then she sees me. Her expression tells me everything I need to know, she's shocked to see me but she's also relieved. People are looking at me like I'm crazy but I don't give a shit. She stands frozen in place just staring at me. I never take my eyes off of her.

Slowly she starts walking towards me, her head down trying to avoid the people openly gawking at us. Minutes later she's standing in front of me, silent and waiting.

"Serena, I'm sorry," I whisper, "You can't go. Not without hearing everything I have to say first."

She says nothing but nods her head to let me know she's listening.

"Since the first day I met you, I knew you were the one for me. I know you feel the same way. You would've picked me. You *should've* picked me. I should have given you that choice. It hurt me to leave you but I swear to you that if you stay, I'll never leave again." Tears begin to form and slowly trickle down her cheeks. I take out the small box with the ring that I've been holding onto for a long time and get down on one knee. "You deserve the world and I want to be the one to give it to you."

I hold my breath as she stares at me.

Serena

Everything has been overwhelming me, the last few weeks have been intense and I've reached my breaking point. My tears stop and instead I feel angry, angry with myself for not seeing what Sean was like sooner and furious for Kaleb for not telling me. Now he has the balls to get down on one knee and hope it'll magically fix everything?

"What the hell Kaleb?" I growl at him, kneeling on the floor in front of me, "Proposing doesn't fix what you did."

"Please, just look Serena. I picked this ring especially for you." There's a look in his eye that I can't ignore. It's pained, almost like he was hurting too. If he hadn't lied to me repeatedly I would believe he was genuinely sorry.

"What—" I shake my head, the ring glinting in the velvet box looks familiar. I lean in and I can't believe it.

"Is that...? How did you get that?" I can barely get my words out, they trip over my tongue.

Two years ago when I was on a shopping trip, I found the most amazing, quaint boutique jewelry shop that specialized in unique pieces. In the window a sapphire white gold ring had caught my eye, it had two small but elegant diamonds either side. I knew I couldn't afford it but I'd gone in anyway. I'd slipped it onto my finger and admired the way the band crossed and intertwined, as if keeping the diamonds safe. I knew it was a mistake because I didn't want to take it off once it was on my hand but I did. I was genuinely a little upset when the sales assistant had put it back in the display cabinet. Sean must have been looking at rings around the same time because he proposed a few weeks later. I touch my finger where my engagement ring used to sit while looking at Kaleb. The one Sean bought me was totally different; it's not something I would have chosen. One giant rock set in a thick gold band; it was flashy, more traditional.

"It was always you Serena. The second I left I knew it was a mistake, but you had a chance at happiness, at the perfect life you wanted." He looks up at me, his blue eyes stormy and sad.

"Jen and I broke up a few months after the move, but we already knew it was over the day we unpacked in our apartment. She wasn't *you*. She started sleeping with someone else and I worked late nights, staying away and driving myself insane with all the things I wish I'd done, wish I'd said."

We've gathered a crowd around us now, people listening in and waiting to see what'll happen. In the distance I can hear the last call for my flight. It's time to make a decision.

"I told myself I had to be fair, I had to give you enough time to see if Sean truly made you happy. So I stayed away. I worked. I existed." He sounds tired and worn down, like he's finally about to come clean about everything and the weight has been lifted. "Then I came into town and I saw you. You looked lost, and I could see that sadness in your eyes even though you smiled. I followed you to the shop and when I saw you put this ring back my heart broke. This ring is yours, it was always meant for you and even if you don't want me, you should have it."

"Two years ago…" I say, trying to process what he's telling me. We could've been together, happy for the last two years but he'd denied us that chance.

"Yes." He replies firmly. I can see a determination on his face. That look he gets when he is willing to risk everything— the one he saves for the boardroom.

"You saw me and you waited this long to come

back?" I still can't believe him and at the same time, I can...He wanted me to be happy with Sean. He thought I was. Kaleb in his own way has tried to look after me, he paid my bills, replaced the money that Sean stole and he tried to shield me from the hurt— a plan that backfired. But the way my heart aches while I look at him, the way I have to fight myself from jumping into his embrace reveals that I love Kaleb. Wholly. Completely. And no matter what he's done to hurt me, I will always love him because he is so ingrained in my soul, he is my other half. Without him I'm incomplete.

"I needed you to be sure. I know that there is no one else out there for me. You are my everything. But I wanted to make sure you felt that way too." He looks defeated now. I can see on his face that he's questioning how I feel about him.

The doubt he's feeling is the one I've been struggling with for weeks and so I decide to let him stew in it a moment longer before I reply, "Yes, you stupid man."

Laura

Epilogue

"Daisy! Daisy come back here." I whisper harshly, looking for my daughter as her blonde hair bobs through the crowds of people milling about. Normally I'd leave her to it, she's a bit like a cat— she'll come back looking for food eventually. But today she'd run off with something important, and very priceless. Something I didn't trust my four year old not to lose in the chaos of today. This wedding had been a year in the planning and I was determined that it would go smoothly.

I pull up the silky fabric that seems to be swimming around my legs and slip off my shoes. Hunting children is an accident waiting to happen and I'm never that stable in heels anyway. I don't know how Daisy got her hands on Serena's grandmothers comb, or what possessed her to take it but I had to find her.

No wait— that was a lie. I knew exactly why she'd taken it; she was going through a shiny 'mine' phase. I couldn't even trust her with tin foil right at the moment. I call out her name again, trying not to draw the attention of any of the guests as I make my way through the house and out into the garden. I can see Kaleb stood near the flower arch in his tux talking to his brother, the sun low in the sky behind him and I sigh. It's all so romantic, and beautiful and something I'll never have. I shake off that lonely thought and take a look around me.

The decorators really have gone all out on Serena's parents place, it looks ethereal. There are white roses everywhere, and glass jars of all shapes and sizes dotted about, each housing a flickering candle. I just want to stop and remember this moment forever, take in how it smells with the roses lingering in the air, how the grass feels beneath my toes, how— I hear a loud crash, followed by a squealing laugh that I know only too well. My spawn is off creating mischief and I need to find her and that damn pearl comb before she ruins my best friend's wedding.

This day had been a long time coming and I wasn't about to let my daughter and her klepto ways postpone it any longer. Serena was going down that aisle in less than twenty minutes, even if I had to get one of Serena's father's fishing nets to catch my feral child.

Following the source of the noise I find myself back in the kitchen, watching several waitresses and the caterer collecting trays off the floor. I exhale, thanking God that they were empty serving trays, not yet loaded with any food.

"Where is she?" I demand and they point me in the direction of the library. I quickly apologize and dash off, hoping to catch her before she knocks anything else over. I have visions of the beautiful four-tier cake smashed on the hardwood floor and my four year old covered in sticky icing.

The library looks empty and I even get down on my hands and knees to look under the desk and the couch to see if she's hiding. That's when I hear angry footsteps behind me.

"Is this yours?" An annoyed voice makes me turn and near his feet I see Daisy, standing there grinning up at him as though he was made of chocolate. Her little pink hand has latched onto his neat grey suit, and she's got a tight hold.

I'm momentarily stunned, not only because Daisy usually hates men but because the gentleman she's latched onto is one of the most handsome men I've ever seen. He has dark hair that just about reaches the collar of his shirt, a strong chiseled jaw with the faintest trace of stubble and a haughty air about him. Remembering his question I crouch down and make myself eye level with my daughter.

"Has she been bothering you?" I ask, offering out to take her hand in mine.

"Yes." He replies curtly, before turning to leave but she still has hold of his trouser leg.

"Yes?" Something about this man sets me on edge. He's rude and arrogant with green eyes that seem to burn right into me. Most people smile and politely say that no, she hadn't been any bother at all but this guy doesn't.

"That's what I said." He says coolly, his gaze never leaving my face. It's like he's trying to rile me up, trying to push my buttons.

"I'm sorry my daughter has so obviously been a nuisance." I'm short with him now, I want him to know I'm angry but I'm refusing to give him a show.

"Either learn to control her or leave her at home next time." He pulls his trousers sharply from her hand.

"Listen here mister, she's the damned flower girl so I won't just 'leave her at home' and as for controlling her— you obviously have no experience with four year olds! You're such a jerk!" I scoop up Daisy, even though she's protesting, reaching out for him with one hand and clasping the comb tightly in the other.

I dash back through the kitchen and upstairs, swiping a cupcake and grabbing my heels on the way. Serena's standing on the landing, a concerned look on her face. Her wedding dress is so perfect for her, simple and figure hugging. She looks amazing in it with her dark hair pinned up, and a loose tendril or two hanging down that I give her a huge goofy grin.

"Is everything okay? You just ran off?" She asks as she puts in her earrings.

"Daisy took your comb, I just went to retrieve it is all." I say, slightly out of breath after the child hunt.

She laughs, well used to my baby's thieving ways by now. She watches with a glint in her eye as I trade the cupcake for the pearl hairpiece. I know she wants a family with Kaleb, something she never saw herself having before. Every time she looks at Daisy I can see how badly she wants it.

I'm so happy for my best friend I feel like I could burst, and as I walk down the aisle behind her, watching her get her happily ever after only the smallest twinge of jealousy gnaws at me. When the priest announces that the groom may now kiss the bride Kaleb cups her face, before bringing his lips to hers in a kiss so scorching it could melt your skin off. I can feel his eyes on me once again as I turn to confirm what I already know, in the front row I spot Mr Arrogant smirking at me.

ACKNOWLEDGEMENTS

Thanks to my boys who are patient with mommy's writing. They are my inspiration everyday – M.S.L.R

Thank you J for always putting up with me and running the house while I hide in my writing cave. I couldn't do it without you – Love, Alice

We want to give Emma our cover designer a huge thank you. You don't seem to realise just how talented you are. You, my lovely, are one special lady!

To A.T. Sullivan, our editor, we're glad you could see where we were heading with this even when it was just patched together in fragments. Thank you for the millions of re-reads you must have done. You're probably sick of Serena and Kaleb by now!

JC Clarke, thank you for doing a fab job with the

formatting and the headings. You were spot on and brilliant as always.

To our Beta Babes, Corinne, Jessica, Beverley, Sherry and Nikki - thank you for helping us take our raw work and polish it up.

Also, thank you to all of the bloggers who signed up to help us spread the word. We hope you guys really enjoyed it and that you stick around for the next book.

ABOUT THE AUTHORS

M.S. L.R.

M.S. L.R., lived in Los Angeles, California for eight years, then moved to Arkansas and has been living there ever since. She graduated Springdale High School in 2007. Currently, she has a full time office job and has two boys that keep her busy when she's not at work or writing romance stories.

She loves to read, write, read and write! Author M.S. L.R. has also published under Stefany Rattles.

Alice La Roux

Alice La Roux is a dirty minded, mouthy Welsh author with an English literature degree who is still trying to find her genre while dabbling in erotica, fantasy and horror. She's a bookworm who reads anything and everything and is addicted to social media. Find her on Twitter @AliLaRoux or see random pictures of her dog and wine over on Instagram @AliceLaRoux. Feel free to add her on Facebook, she doesn't bite…much.